Just the Way You Are

Allison M. Lewis

Copyright ©2015, Allison M. Lewis

All rights reserved. No part of this publication may be reproduced, stored in a retrieval system, or transmitted in any form or by any means, electronic, mechanical, photocopying, recording, or otherwise, without the prior written permission of the publisher.

Printed in the United States of America

♥ *This story is dedicated to Dylan Boot, whose love for me inspired much of it. Thank you for loving and accepting me just the way I am, sweetie!* ♥

Acknowledgements

Firstly, I would like to acknowledge Erin Haney. After proving herself to be an invaluable asset throughout the process of editing my Master's thesis, she once again came through for me when it was time to edit this story. Thank you so much! I appreciate your help so much more than I can say.

Secondly, I would like to acknowledge Erin Kelly. Not only is she one of my best friends in the entire world, but she is also an amazing editor. I cannot thank her enough for the time she spent editing this story. I will always be grateful. Thank you so much, Erin! You will always be my fellow Raider and sister.

Thirdly, I would like to acknowledge my personal assistant, Angelique "Angie" Washington. She spent countless nights listening while I complained about long days of writing or of not writing throughout the completion of this endeavor. Thank you so much, Angie! I could not have finished this story without your continuous encouragement.

Additionally, I would like to acknowledge my mother, Kimberly Hughes. She encouraged me to try wheelchair ballet as a teenager, which subsequently led to my lifelong love of dance. Perhaps more importantly, she persuaded me to dance as a butterfly in a performance of *A Midsummer Night's Dream*. This was an exceptional experience that I will remember for the rest of my life; it also provided one of the themes for this story. Most notably, though, my mother has always told me that I can do anything I set my mind to.

Last, but certainly not least, I'd like to acknowledge my boyfriend, Dylan Boot. I am not sure I would have started writing again after graduate school had he not kept urging me to do so. Thanks so much for your support throughout this whole process, sweetie!

Contents

Chapter One 9
Chapter Two 17
Chapter Three 21
Chapter Four 32
Chapter Five 43
Chapter Six 52
Chapter Seven 62
Chapter Eight 72
Chapter Nine 81
Chapter Ten 89
Chapter Eleven 101
Chapter Twelve 107
Chapter Thirteen 121
Chapter Fourteen 128
About the Author 135

Chapter One

Once upon a time, in a faraway land called Starryton, there lived a princess named Misty. Like many other princesses before her, she was loved and adored by her subjects and doted upon by her parents. The citizens of Starryton often gushed over her skin, which resembled that of dolls frequently displayed in curio cabinets. She wondered, however, if they would still gush if they ever realized what separated her from the other princesses of the world: her wheelchair.

Misty had been in a wheelchair since she was very young because she had a disability that left her unable to walk or properly use both of her hands. This disability had been kept a secret in Starryton for as long as she could remember because her father didn't want the royal family to appear weak to the people of the kingdom. For years her parents kept her comfortable, but hidden, in the highest tower of their castle.

Misty had the best of everything and the nicest help. This included Dex, a Labrador retriever as black as coal yet as soft as velvet; he was her service dog and the apple of her eye. Despite Dex's company, Misty couldn't help but feel like a cross between Rapunzel and Ariel because she was hidden from a world she desperately wished to be a part of. She loved her parents and understood that they were only trying to protect the life they had always known. She was getting old by princess standards, though, and she wished to find love.

Truth be told, she'd loved Prince Derrick of Mooncrest, the neighboring kingdom, from afar for years. He loved to dance and was known for being as graceful as a gazelle prancing through the forest when he did. His gentle nature and caring heart had also earned him a reputation as one of the kindest people for miles around. Once, Misty had seen his picture in the *Starryton Gazette* because he'd saved an elderly courtier, giving her CPR after a dance lesson gone wrong. Misty had spent countless hours since that night fantasizing about how he would fall in love with her in an instant if they ever danced, but she knew this could never happen unless her parents allowed her to leave her tower and join the world. She'd had several conversations with them about this over the years, to no avail, but her failures didn't stop her from making yet another attempt on the eve of her twenty-first birthday as they all sat at the table together to have a celebratory dinner.

"I've decided what I want for my birthday." She flashed her father, Reginald, what she hoped was a cute, innocent smile.

The snowy white-haired, pot-bellied king chuckled and gave her mother, Eliza, a knowing look. "Better get some coins ready, darling."

Misty rolled her eyes. "You underestimate me, Daddy. What I want this year doesn't cost a thing." Taking a bite of a chicken tender, she waited for him to process what she'd said before continuing with her request. "I want to spend the day outside, leave the tower, so I can explore Starryton."

The moment the princess finished, her mother sighed and hung her head, holding her face between her hands. "Not this again."

Misty mirrored Eliza's posture, frustrated by the fact that this all-too-familiar argument had once again made the usually larger-than-life, silver-haired woman look so very small.

The king stood up from the table then, the way his forehead wrinkled exposing both his age and his anger. "Why do you insist on constantly indulging in the fantasies of a young girl?" he huffed in frustration. "I've told you time and time again that we can never grant a ridiculous request such as this."

Misty readied herself for a fight and internally coached herself not to back down. "What I want is far from ridiculous, Daddy. I'm sick of being cooped up in this tower. I'll be 21 years old tomorrow and I want to see the world," she pleaded.

"I don't care how old you are!" the king's face reddened, the wrinkles in his forehead becoming deeper as he started to rant. "You're my daughter. Your mother and I need you here. Doesn't that mean anything to you?"

Tears welling in her eyes, Misty struggled to answer. "Of course it does, but you can't shelter me forever. You have to understand how much I want to see the world."

The king shook his head. "No. No, no, no. It's too great a risk. We can't just let you aimlessly wander the kingdom. There's no telling what people would do or say," he explained, his face becoming more flushed with every word.

"There it is. There's the truth!" Misty shouted as the tears she'd been holding back finally spilled from her eyes. "You're ashamed of me and afraid of others' opinions." She sniffled as another flood of tears burned behind her eyes.

Before the king could respond, the queen lifted her head, revealing her own tears to Misty and her husband. "Sweetheart, please understand; your father and I aren't ashamed of you. We only want to protect you, and we can't do that if you go out into the kingdom because we have no control over what will happen or the impact your journey will have on the monarchy."

"The monarchy, the monarchy, the monarchy. I'm sick of hearing about the stupid monarchy. I'm your daughter! I should be more important than any monarchy!" she shouted, still crying.

Her father let out another angry huff before resuming his argument. "You aren't listening to me or your mother. We have to protect you in order to protect the monarchy. Your going out into the kingdom is far too dangerous. It could put our family's reputation, as well as its future, at risk. I cannot allow that." The authority with which the king spoke should have frightened her, but it didn't. It only made her angrier.

"For crying out loud, Daddy! You're not listening to me, either. What about my future? What about my happiness? Doesn't that matter to you?"

Her father looked at her for a long moment, and she noticed his face hadn't lost any of its earlier redness. "You are my daughter. I am, first and foremost, your father, yes. But, as king, I must always be thinking of the good of the realm along with everything else. People discovering the truth about you is just too much of a liability. It could give them ideas and they could try to take the right to rule from us before your cousin can step in and take my throne."

At that moment, all Misty wanted was to ask why she couldn't take the throne when it was time for her father to step down; it was her birthright, after all. She knew that adding that to the fight would take it to even scarier heights because neither she nor her parents were ready to face the answer to that question. She knew deep down that her father believed that there was no way she could reign over Starryton because of her disability, but she wasn't prepared to hear him admit it out loud. Before she could put all these thoughts into one coherent response, her mother spoke.

"Misty, darling, your father and I both desperately want you to be happy, but we don't see any way of giving you what you want while still protecting the kingdom and the future of this family. Please, please, understand," the queen said, sadness permeating her voice.

Despite the deep anguish her parents were displaying, for a moment, Misty felt a glimmer of hope. "What if there was a way to do both? A way to allow me to see the world and protect the monarchy at the same time?"

"What do you mean?" Confusion was written in her parents' features as two voices asked one question.

Misty smiled ever so slightly through the tears that hadn't stopped falling. "I don't necessarily have to explore *this* kingdom. I could explore another kingdom, one where people won't know me. Our neighbor kingdom of Mooncrest is an option."

"Absolutely not. I would never allow such a thing. Ever!" the king bellowed, a large vein in his forehead becoming visible and his face going from red to almost purple with the force of the words. "The real reason you want to leave is clear now. It has nothing to do with wanting to see the world. All you want to do is meet that stupid boy you talk about incessantly, disgracing your family in the process." He let out a single angry chuckle. "Well, that's not going to happen. You are never to leave this tower for any reason, let alone to explore this kingdom or any other. That is an order." Her father stomped away from the table and slammed the door that led to the castle proper behind him.

Her mother could only shake her head in horror and cry with renewed emotion as she watched the king leave. "How could you even think of doing this to the family?" she asked, as she wiped away her tears with a finger.

The princess wished she could reason with her mother and explain once again that she wished to focus more on her personal happiness than that of the realm. She wanted to point out that the possibility of disgracing the family hadn't even crossed her mind when this brilliant plan was created. But, before she could even utter a syllable, the queen ran after the king, still sobbing.

* * *

Misty sat in her tower for a while after her parents left, replaying the argument in her mind. She eventually sighed, coming to the conclusion that she would never be able to please her parents and fulfill her true desires.

Dex walked over and placed his head in her lap, as though he sensed her sadness and wanted to remind her of his presence.

"Hey, bud." She offered him the slightest of smiles as she petted his head. "So sorry you had to hear us fight again. I should have guessed this was going to happen. If there's anyone in the world they really want to keep me from, it's him." She chuckled halfheartedly, tears dotting Dex's fur as she continued to pet him and think about how ironic her request was.

She'd had a crush on Derrick for years; the irony of her urge to explore his kingdom lay not in this, but in the fact that Mooncrest and Starryton had once formed the united kingdom of Starrycrest.

Taking things a step further, for years, Misty and Derrick's families had practically been one entity due, in part, to Derrick's grandfather having been *her* grandfather's trusted second in command, often helping to resolve conflict in the land. As a result, her father and Derrick's father, Archibald, had grown up as friends and both happened to be promising chefs as teenagers. Their friendship irrevocably dissolved, and, consequently, the kingdom was torn apart by a cooking competition that determined the land's official chef. Misty could still remember how frustrated her father had gotten the couple of times she'd heard him speak about it. "It was entirely too unrealistic," he'd say. "No self-respecting chef can make a dish meant for a king in 30 minutes. And let me tell you something else: only your grandfather could have thought of something that crazy."

Misty figured that her father called the competition unrealistic because, not only were competitors given only a half hour to make their dishes, they were also required to use no ingredients other than those chosen by the king. These remained a mystery to the competitors until the start of each day's challenge. According to the majority of the people present for the event, neither teen was surprised when they were presented with the makings of a perfect chocolate cupcake, the king's favorite dessert, as the final task.

Misty laughed to herself, continuing to pet Dex on the head as she recalled how dramatic her father had acted the few times he'd shared his version of the tale. Even though it had happened years before she was born, she could perfectly picture her father's proud expression falling the moment the king became ill after eating the confection he'd been so confident about. Worse yet, she could see his beet-red expression and the anger that filled his eyes when her grandfather decided to name Archibald the official chef of the kingdom over his own son; she'd seen his features set in a similar way many times. However, she couldn't begin to imagine the extent of her father's rage after it was discovered that vanilla, which the king happened to be allergic to, was somehow put into the batter he'd mixed. Although she understood why he did so, Misty wished her father hadn't been so quick to accuse Archibald of committing the crime. It was this accusation that ignited a feud between the two families, a rift which ultimately led to their inability to effectively govern together and the creation of two individual realms.

In spite of the toxic history between their families, Misty had felt an instant connection with Derrick the moment she noticed his picture. She figured because she was about to be 21 and enter adulthood by Starryton standards, there was no better time than now to explore this attraction, even if it meant going against her parents' wishes and dealing with the consequences. At the stroke of midnight, she quietly transferred from her bed to her wheelchair, packed a bag with clothes, all of the tools necessary to style her hair, as well as her favorite silver sequin covered butterfly-shaped novelty handbag, and snuck out of the castle; Dex trailing silently behind her. A troll who granted wishes for a price was rumored to live deep in an untraveled portion of the land. Misty decided she was going to request that she have the ability to walk and dance in addition to becoming as breathtaking as a setting sunset. This was what the other princesses of the world had been given, she reasoned, and she wanted to have it too.

Misty and Dex made it to the troll's hut at the edge of the forest within three hours. Taking a steadying breath and touching Dex's cold black nose to reassure him as he came to a stop beside her, she entered the hut and cleared her throat to get the troll's attention. To Misty's surprise, the troll greatly resembled the treasure trolls she'd loved and spent hours playing with as a little girl. The only differences lay in the fact that this particular troll, known as Trovella, was taller than a skyscraper, most likely weighed more than a sumo wrestler, had hair and a gemstone as black as night, and looked as though a smile hadn't graced her face in 500 years.

Chapter Two

"Who dares darken the doorway of my hut at such an early hour?" the troll's voice was thick and raspy, but she still somehow managed to yell.

"The princess of Starryton," answered Misty, her voice a squeak as she rolled into the light.

"My dear child, I see why you've come to me. I only wonder what took you so long," Trovella said in a condescending tone as she eyed Misty's wheelchair disdainfully.

"Yes, Trovella, I have hidden my true self from the kingdom for years. I have decided, from this day forward, to hide no longer. I wish for nothing more than to be able to walk and dance like a graceful angel so that Prince Derrick of Mooncrest will fall in love with me," she declared wistfully, her eyes sparkling with love.

"Young love is so beautiful," Trovella growled sarcastically, glaring at the princess with even more revulsion following this revelation.

Sensing Trovella's disgust, Misty pleaded, "Trovella, give me what I desire and I'll do anything—I can pay you any sum."

An evil laugh escaped Trovella's mouth, but she stopped short of smiling. "Dear, dear child. Don't worry your pretty little head. I'm certain we can make a deal."

Misty sat up straighter, feeling a bit more confident. "Name your terms."

Her chuckles following her as she moved, Trovella disappeared into the back of the hut and came back a moment later with a necklace.

Misty examined the necklace with awe. It was understated in comparison to most of her royal jewelry, but still impressive. A dainty gold chain held a three-layer pendant featuring a rich red ruby on top, followed by a shiny golden topaz, and finished with a stunning blue sapphire.

"The precious stones in this necklace have the power to grant your wish, child, but it will only become a reality for a limited time unless the prince does fall for you," Trovella informed her.

"Oh, he'll fall for me. He will. I know he will," Misty responded eagerly, reaching for the necklace.

Trovella shook her head and pulled it away. "Not so fast, dear child. I must first tell you the terms of our deal. In exchange for this gift, I would like the gems from your tiara."

Misty gasped. She'd forgotten she was even wearing the piece they were discussing. Having the diamond and sapphire studded tiara nestled in her hair had always been second nature to her—she could put it on without assistance. She knew that, without crown jewels, no one would believe she was royalty, not even Derrick, but she wanted him to fall for who she was, not her status. She loved the tiara and it had been in her family for three generations but, as hard as it was, she took the jeweled headpiece from its perch and examined it for a moment before finally handing it to the troll.

"Thank you, my dear," Trovella whispered unsympathetically. "I know with a little help from this," she gestured at the silver in her hand, "I will grant the greatest of wishes."

In the next breath, the troll extended both of her arms out in front of her like she was going to throw a fireball towards Misty but, instead of fire, the princess felt a jolt. Before she could even utter a syllable, she realized the necklace that Trovella had been holding was now around her neck. The troll laughed yet again, but the sound still had no hint of humor.

"Beautiful, isn't it?" she hissed, her voice dripping with sarcasm. "Now, to the details. If you make the prince fall in love with you in three days, the wish will become permanent. Simply put, you and Princey will live happily ever after while I hold on to your crown." The troll scoffed, as if to say *that's never going to happen*, before her expression turned stern. "But, if you don't, your wish will reverse and you must declare, by royal decree, that I can stop granting wishes and live freely in the land." The troll's tone, though still mocking, did nothing to hide her excitement at the prospect of freedom.

Misty bit her lip in an effort to avoid laughing at Trovella's request. She knew it was absurd; there was also the issue of her father being furious if this ended badly and Trovella was released. Her instinct was confirmed when Dex began circling her frantically and giving her a despondent look that pled with her not to agree. She ignored the dog completely; she had to take a chance at personal happiness.

"It's a deal," she breathed quietly, her voice cracking slightly from nervousness.

"Excellent!" An evil gleam sparkled in Trovella's eye.

The moment Misty agreed, a bright purple light surrounded her and she felt another sharp jolt, much stronger than the one she'd felt moments before, work its way through her body from head to toe. Her disability had made her immune to the occasional muscle spasm, but this vibration felt like a thousand little muscle contractions at once. She held back a scream, relieved that the pain proved to be momentary. As her muscles relaxed, she smiled, feeling a difference even within seconds of the transformation; her body had more control and, thus, her confidence was bolstered. A moment later, she took a deep breath and hesitantly stood up. She chose a spot directly in front of her wheelchair in case she needed somewhere to fall but, to her utter delight, she did not. She smiled from ear to ear and took two steps towards Dex, whose eyes were as big as saucers. When this movement was successful as well, she burst into excited sing-songy laughter.

"Perfect, my fair child," Trovella praised, her features still appearing wicked as she made another trip to the back of the hut.

The troll returned quickly, holding a jewel-studded phonograph that sparkled more than any stone Misty had ever seen. "Now for the final test!" Trovella bellowed after turning the device on.

As soon as a song, just as beautiful as the one programmed into nearly every music box across the kingdom, filled the hut, Misty danced, performing pliés and pirouettes as easily as she breathed.

Trovella's maniacal countenance became even more pronounced as she turned off the phonograph and looked at Misty. "You are ready, dear child. Remember. You have exactly three days. One of the necklace's stones will turn into an opal every day at sunset as a reminder," she said as the fireball Misty had expected to feel moments before suddenly engulfed her wheelchair. "If the prince isn't in love with you by the time the sun sets on the third day, your wish will reach its end and our agreement will go into effect." The troll's face twisted hideously with each word.

Misty continued to stand, despite the fact that she could have been knocked over with the slightest touch of a feather, as she watched her wheelchair and the fireball surrounding it disappear. "Understood. And th—" she began.

"Be gone now. I've got wishes to grant," Trovella sighed, rolling her eyes.

With that, Misty motioned for Dex to follow and the two of them walked out into the early morning light to find the prince.

Chapter Three

"So, Dex, what do you think I should say to the prince? I can't just come out and say I like him. He has to fall for me, so maybe I should dance in the village square or bring him some food. Mama does always say the way to a man's heart is through his stomach."

Before long, Misty heard barking in the distance and realized that Dex was no longer listening to her, but had decided to chase a cockatoo around the moat of Prince Derrick's castle instead.

"Dex, what are you doing? Come back here!" Misty was surprised how effortlessly her legs broke into a run as she went after him.

As she reached the moat, she noticed that not only was Dex chasing the poor bird, he was also trying to eat it.

"Stop! Dex, stop," she yelled as he snapped his teeth at the screeching ball of feathers. When he didn't listen, she grabbed his collar to pull him away. Unfortunately, at that exact moment, Dex jerked forward, pulling Misty and catapulting her into the water.

Misty screamed because, even though she could now walk and dance, she still didn't have any idea how to swim. She didn't have many options, so she kicked and thrashed her arms and legs, trying to stay afloat. "Help, help! Please, somebody help me!" she cried. To Misty's amazement, Prince Derrick came almost out of thin air, dove into the moat, and was pulling her out in a flash.

His arms were stronger than she ever dreamed they would be and they left her feeling impossibly safe. It was seeing his incredible eyes in person, orbs made up of a brighter and richer blue than the fourth layer of a rainbow, which paralyzed her in an unbelievable way as he carried her to a nearby bench, sat her down gently, and slid into the spot next to her.

"Are you okay, miss?" he asked, his face wrinkled with concern. "I was taking a walk to clear my head and I heard you screaming."

Dex barked, making Misty, who'd gone mute staring into the eyes of the prince, snap back to reality.

"Oh, yes! Thank you so much for saving my life. I'm sorry if I disturbed you. It's just that D-Dex—," Misty pointed toward the dog as her teeth started to chatter.

"It's okay. You're okay," Derrick murmured, his voice soft and sweet.

Smiling, Misty took a deep breath, and told him how she had fallen into the moat trying to save a cockatoo from Dex's jaws.

Derrick laughed when she finished the story. "Are you referring to those guys?" he pointed towards Dex and the cockatoo, who were now peacefully sitting next to each other beside the moat.

"Uh—Yes, that would be them," Misty admitted, shock coloring her features.

Derrick chuckled again. "Well, it looks like they worked it out. Nevertheless, you did attempt to save the life of Cliff, my cockatoo, so the least I can do is offer you a hot meal and dry clothes." He smiled, exposing pearly white teeth.

Seeing Derrick's smile, the princess thought she might faint but, by some miracle, she managed to stay alert and upright. "No, no. Thank you, but I couldn't. I know that you're a prince and everything, but I don't even know you."

The prince nodded at this, his grin still in place. "I'm Derrick. And you are?"

"Misty," she replied nervously, holding out her hand.

"You're not like other girls, are you?" he shook his head, amused, as he did the same with her hand. "There, we've been introduced. Now come on into the castle. Dex too."

"Are you sure?" Misty asked.

Derrick took her hand in his. "C'mon, before I have to order you into the castle by royal decree," he teased.

Then he led her into the castle, their furry and feathered sidekicks following close behind.

As soon as they entered Derrick's home, Misty was overwhelmed by it. Her family's castle was vintage, well kept, and beautiful in its own right, but Derrick's castle was modern and meticulously decorated with pink and purple orchids inside and out.

"What a beautiful place."

"Thank you. The queen is partial to orchids." Derrick's lips quirked upward affectionately as he mentioned his mother.

Another smile so soon after the first made Misty's heart skip a beat. She once again managed to stay conscious and focused, but zeroed in on the floor so he wouldn't see her blush.

"Do you mind if I go dry off in the washroom?" she asked timidly, shifting her weight from one foot to the other.

Derrick chuckled sweetly. "I'll do you one better. Wait right here." He disappeared down a corridor, emerging a moment later with a beautiful emerald gown. "Why don't you change into this and then come to the dining hall and join me for supper?"

Misty could no longer hide her blush as it deepened and her cheeks became hot. "You've done so much already. I couldn't impo—"

Derrick cut her off with a shake of his head. "It's no imposition. Cliff and I insist that you and Dex join us for the evening."

"Won't your parents mind that you've invited a random stranger to dinner?" she asked, her voice shaking a little, wordlessly willing him not to take back his offer.

"We've already established that we're no longer strangers," Derrick admonished. "Besides, my parents are away. Traveling. They won't be back until my mother's birthday, which isn't for a few more weeks. Please stay for dinner so I have something to look forward to." The prince flashed her a bright grin, holding the outfit out to her in invitation.

Derrick's smile once again left a flutter in her chest. In an effort to be polite, Misty nodded hesitantly, accepted the dress, and agreed to meet him in an hour; she didn't give her rational mind any time to talk her heart out of this plan.

* * *

Biting her lip as she examined herself in the mirror of the washroom, Misty sighed.

She'd been inundated with nerves ever since she'd figured out that an hour was not enough time to get ready as well as style her hair—prior to tonight, she'd always had help with the physical demands in this department, thanks to her lack of motor skills. *I wish I had thought about these things before I made my wish,* she thought. Standing in front of the mirror, she let out an angry huff. *How pathetic am I? I was given an incredible miracle that I'm not appreciating and I already want to amend it.* Disgusted with these notions, she shook her head and, in that moment, decided she would push through situations like this from now on, taking full advantage of the gift she'd gotten.

As she struggled to remove the soaked dress she was wearing, she added another layer to the realization that getting herself ready was harder than she'd ever thought it would be, even with the benefit of two hands.

She got her dress off, pulled the dry gown over her head, pushed her arms through the sleeves, and yanked it the rest of the way down. Studying her appearance in the mirror, she smiled, grateful that she'd managed to change her clothes without breaking anything or hurting herself. Her happiness disappeared in an instant, though, as she became aware that her preoccupation with the logistics of changing had left little room to realize that her signature updo, a tight, neat bun, closely resembled a wet mop.

Taking her hair down quickly, she considered trying to redo her bun. She'd told her assistants exactly how to style her hair every day for more than a decade, so she was fairly sure she could handle it. The only problem was that the end of her hour to get cleaned up was rapidly approaching. She needed, and wanted, to use every minute she had with the prince to her advantage and this left her no time to search through the bag she'd packed, carefully choosing the perfect styling materials which consisted of a comb, two hair ties, a scrunchie, and a bottle of a tried and true hairspray appropriately named The Royal Treatment. Instead, she toweled her hair for ten seconds, drying it as much as possible, and brushed her fingers through it when this was done. As a last touch, Misty checked her entire ensemble in the mirror and concluded that she resembled old pictures she'd found of her mother over the years. In her youth, the queen had loved to crimp her hair, an affinity that Misty had, however unconsciously, inherited.

Thinking of her mother led Misty to contemplate her father and how angry he would be once he learned that she'd run away; her brain choosing to go through this cycle at this moment only increased her anxiety. Knowing she had to compose herself if she was going to be able to spend time with Derrick without bursting into tears, she focused her gaze on the marble of the sink, grabbed her handbag knowing that no formal ensemble was complete without it, took a couple deep breaths, gave her reflection a nod, and walked into the hall.

To her surprise, upon her arrival at her destination, Derrick poked his head in from the kitchen. He opened his mouth to say something, then closed it without speaking, smiling absent-mindedly. If she didn't think it was too soon for this to happen, in that moment, she would've said he was in love with her.

She smiled back, an awkward silence settling in the space between them.

"Have a drink," he said, bringing their long pause to an end, tilting his head toward a table lit with candles and holding a bottle of apple cider and two champagne flutes. "Dinner will be ready in five minutes."

Pouring herself a glass, Misty examined the romantic scene before her, happier than she'd been in her entire life. She was so lost in her own world that she was startled when the prince returned after a while and served her a plate of chicken, asparagus, and mashed potatoes before sitting across from her with his own plate of food.

"Bon appètit!" he offered, before biting into a piece of the meat.

"Everything looks delicious," she commented, catching her bottom lip between her teeth so she wouldn't divulge her hatred of vegetables.

"Perhaps you should try something before you say that," Derrick laughed. "My staff is off for the weekend. I made it myself, so if it's horrible, please lie."

Misty's eyes went wide. She adored the fact that, like her, he was humble enough to permit his staff the occasional day off. "So. The prince cooks, huh?"

"Yes, I slaved over a hot stove just for you." Derrick wiped his brow, feigning exhaustion.

Misty giggled. "Well, if that's the case, I must try it." After inspecting her chicken critically, she hesitantly picked up her fork and cut into it. Slowly bringing the bite to her mouth, she noticed, at the last second, that the chicken was filled with spinach. She swallowed it anyway; there was no turning back now.

"Wow. This is actually really good!" she exclaimed when she'd had time to reflect on what she'd just eaten.

"Should I be flattered or shocked by your glowing recommendation? I'll have to ask the king if he's ever received similar accolades." Derrick laughed.

A smile lit up Misty's face. "The king taught you how to cook? Like father, like son." She wanted to sound casual in spite of the nerves that had wormed into her as she was reminded of the history between their families.

Derrick's face fell and he stared down at his plate for a moment. "No, actually. I taught myself how to cook," he explained quietly. "Although Dad is a fabulous chef, he hasn't cooked in years. Out of necessity, I am a self-taught culinary professional." Lifting his head, the prince looked at her thoughtfully.

Sensing he had more to add, Misty smiled sweetly at him and stayed quiet.

"I enjoy cooking, but not as much as my father did. It was his passion, but years ago a contest came between him and his best friend. He hasn't cooked anything since," Derrick said solemnly.

"I'm so sorry to hear that," she told him, her voice soft and kind. A wave of sadness washed over her as she recognized the profound impact the cooking competition had had on both of their families. She needed there to be a way for her to fix the situation.

"Thank you. I know it probably seems stupid, but the fact that my father gave up on his dream takes away a little of the hope I have for the future," he elaborated solemnly. "I'm as passionate about dancing as he once was about cooking. I can't imagine giving it up, but what if I do? I still don't fully understand why he gave up, and I need to. I can't afford to follow in his footsteps on this."

Misty fidgeted in her chair, suddenly uncomfortable; she knew more about their families' saga than the prince did. "It's not stupid. It means that you love your father. Why don't you tell me more about dancing?" Inwardly, she cringed at the weak attempt to change the subject.

As lame as the segue might have been, it succeeded in putting the prince in an enthusiastic mood, and they spent the rest of the evening chatting easily over their dinner and a delicately prepared dessert of chocolate-covered strawberries. Just as day was turning to night, a clap of thunder pulled them out of their comfortable bubble.

Misty jumped at the noise as Dex ran to her side, whimpering. She stroked his soft coat protectively, her embarrassment at how thunder left her just as scared causing a flush to settle on her face. This deepened when it became clear that Derrick had taken her hand.

"It's okay," he soothed, squeezing her hand reassuringly as Cliff, not wanting to miss any action, landed on his shoulder.

They all sat in silence as they listened to the clatter of the storm until Derrick spoke, keeping hold of her hand. "You'll stay here tonight. I'll prepare one of the extra bedrooms for you."

Misty began to protest, but switched to a hushed, "Thank you…," halfway through. She offered to help him with whatever he needed to do in the room, but he insisted that she make herself at home and explore the castle with Dex. Then he presented her with a flowing purple nightgown.

"For such a gentleman, you have an absurd amount of ladies' clothing," she joked, accepting the sleepwear happily.

The prince winked. "I assure you, madam, you're the only female guest I've had in quite some time. My sister happened to leave a few unnecessary garments here after she married."

Misty laid her hand on his shoulder. "In that case, I commend you for being brave enough to go through your sister's closet." Her laugh echoed behind her as she returned to the washroom she'd used earlier. After another hour-long struggle to wrestle her body into the nightgown and make herself presentable, Misty and Dex wandered the castle. They had visited, and instantly fallen in love with, every room—from the movie theater to the dance studio—when she heard him searching for her.

"Derrick?" she called, walking back through the castle with Dex at her heels, following his voice.

His "in here…," was the final breadcrumb she needed to reveal that he was in his father's den.

Her breath caught as she saw that he'd laid blankets, two pillows, and a dog's squeaky toy in front of the fireplace. "For Dex." He smiled warmly as she and the topic of conversation walked in. "Will this work?"

"Will it work? Will it work!?!" she repeated incredulously. "Of course it will. It's—lovely." Misty watched Dex trot to the pillows and stretch, getting acquainted with the space. "Thank you so much," she whispered as she covered Dex with the blanket he wasn't laying on.

Derrick kneeled next to her, a willing spectator to the way she lovingly petted Dex's head. "Come and see your room," he murmured when she had finished tucking her companion in for the evening.

They walked down two long corridors in pleasant silence before he opened the door to her beautiful room, boasting cherry furnishings and tulips adding stylish touches to the décor. These ranged from brightly colored paintings on the focal wall to a bud-shaped vase, filled with three of the pink variety, on the nightstand. Even though the entire room was elegant, it was the canopy bed accented with the fluffiest pillows Misty had ever come across that stole her attention. Emotion rendered her speechless, and she had to actively resist the urge to jump up and down on the bed like an excited schoolgirl—something she'd always wanted to do, but never had the ability.

"Each room in the castle is decorated using a different flower. I chose this room for you because tulips are my favorite flower. I hope you like it," he said quietly.

Misty looked at him and smiled, searching for words. "I love it, thank you. It's gorgeous!" she exclaimed.

Derrick beamed then quickly shifted his gaze away from her. "So are you," he exhaled under his breath.

She turned to face him. "Hmmm?"

The prince shrugged away her question, pulling down the covers for her. "Hop in." He swept his hand in the direction of the crisp, thick sheets.

Misty kept her excitement in check, getting into bed as gracefully as she could.

"Thank you so much for everything," she breathed sweetly.

He grinned in reply as he pulled up the blankets and started to tuck her in. After a second, he stopped abruptly. "You left your necklace on."

"Oops," The princess fingered the item nervously before admitting, "I didn't even notice."

"You shouldn't sleep with it on. I can't have a beautiful lady strangling in her sleep under my roof," Derrick said nervously.

Misty's blush came back with a vengeance as she realized he expected her to take off the necklace on her own. She'd always had help with activities like putting on makeup or jewelry because she couldn't get her lone usable hand to cooperate enough to accomplish them alone. She also wasn't sure the necklace would even come off, considering Trovella had put it on with magic. Despite these uncertainties, she knew that she had to at least give it a try, given that she finally had full movement in both hands. She took a deep breath, forced her features into positivity mode, found the clasp, and made an effort to undo it. She gave the task all of her strength, but the clasp remained closed. After a couple of minutes, the prince stepped in.

"Here, let me." Gently putting his arms around her neck, he unhooked the clasp in no time at all.

He admired the necklace for a minute before carefully placing it on the vanity. "It's breathtaking," he complimented.

Misty's face brightened. "Thank you. For everything," she responded sweetly.

"My pleasure." His features illuminated to match hers as he tightened the sheets around her and smoothed a wrinkle out of the comforter.

She held her breath; he was reluctant to leave and, as a result, stalling. She lost almost all the air in her lungs when he kissed her forehead, whispered "sweet dreams," and left the room without another word.

Misty had complete confidence in the wish she had made, and the fact that it would remain in effect forever. As she fell asleep that night, it was to this unassailable truth and of a dream of her long-awaited prince, Derrick.

Chapter Four

The smell of molten chocolate woke Misty just as the first beams of light began to break through her window the next morning. She sat up in the bed, rubbed her eyes, and smiled as she remembered the previous day.

A moment later, Derrick knocked lightly on her door before entering carrying a serving tray.

"Good morning, I come bearing sustenance," he greeted cheerfully.

"I hope they're as delicious as I assume they'll be. I love chocolate." She looked down at the plate of chocolate chip waffles in front of her, delighted

"Good! I was counting on it. Dex wasn't exactly forthcoming with clues as to what your go-to breakfast is," he joked. "Also. You mentioned last night that you like to dance, right?"

Misty nodded eagerly, taking her first bite of breakfast as she did.

His lips curved upward. "In that case, enjoy your food, put this leotard on, and meet me in the studio." To complement these instructions, he handed over a lavender leotard, complete with shiny sequins that were a shade darker.

"Is that an order?" she laughed dryly before spearing another mouthful.

"I never make royal decrees on Saturday mornings, but I'm hoping you'll spend the day with me anyway," he elaborated kindly before leaping theatrically out of the room, making her dissolve into laughter.

Misty did her best to get ready quickly, but the more she hurried to dress and alleviate her bedhead, the longer it took her. It took only a short time for her to learn that, even though leotards were somewhat stretchy, the process of donning one wasn't any easier because of this. After killing herself putting it on, she still had to tackle her hair. Misty retrieved two hair ties and a scrunchie from the bag she'd packed to simplify things, stood in front of the mirror and pulled her hair into the bun she'd asked her personal assistants to create a million times. Catching sight of the end result, she saw that her bun was a near-exact copy of the disaster that yesterday's spill into the moat had created, and she frowned. Pushing her failure aside, she settled on wrangling her hair into a simple ponytail in order to avoid wasting precious daylight. To her dismay, even this took several minutes. When she finally finished, she found herself running to the studio to meet the prince and having to stop short of stepping over the threshold. Derrick's graceful flexibility mesmerized her. She was captivated not only by his elegance and precision, but also by the look of ecstasy on his face as he performed. *I hope I am that happy someday*, she thought as she stared at him.

As much as she wanted to step into the room and dance with him, she could not tear her eyes away from his tall, handsome frame and chiseled muscles long enough to move.

"Hi there." He waved a hand in front of her face to get her attention; she'd been staring so intensely that he'd noticed.

"You're quite the dancer."

Derrick nodded in thanks. "What about you? Have any moves?"

"I've got moves like you've never seen," Misty giggled, her cheeks tinting crimson as it occurred to her that, until yesterday, her 'moves' consisted of spinning circles in her wheelchair doing doughnuts until they made her dizzy.

"Okay, that settles it," Derrick teased brightly. "I demand to be dazzled."

Misty laughed as he walked over to his phonograph and turned the volume up. *I bet he would enjoy Trovella's jewel-studded one*, the princess mused as she took in his antiquated, less stunning machine.

"I can't believe you use a phonograph." Her voice was filled with wonder. "Why don't you just hire a harpist or pianist?"

The prince shook his head in protest. "What can I say? I'm old school. My family has had this for years. I like what I know, I guess."

"How lo—" Misty began.

Derrick moved his head from side to side again. "Nope. No more changing the subject. You're supposed to be dazzling me. I order you to do so. I am going to make an exception to my Saturday rule and decree it." He shrugged, grinning from ear to ear.

"Oh, the pressure's really on now." The constant heat in her cheeks intensified. She badly wanted to impress him, but knew that his expertise extended far beyond pliés and pirouettes. Suddenly, the fairies' lullaby from her favorite ballet, *A Midsummer Night's Dream*, during which beautiful dancers buzzed around the stage as tantalizing sprites, came to mind and she wanted nothing more than to dance as stunningly and delicately as those women. To her disbelief, no sooner did she make this silent plea than the movements performed over the course of this routine entered her consciousness. As the music played, she executed each movement with harmonious, precise fluidity, her body the most delicate instrument ever crafted. She finished with a last flourish and a faraway expression, nervously awaiting Derrick's opinion.

"Is that all?" he asked after a moment.

Ending the music with a touch of her hand, Misty made her way over to Derrick and playfully knocked him upside his head. "What do you mean, 'is that all'?"

The prince couldn't keep a straight face, his eyes betraying him and twinkling with glee. "I'm kidding! That was wonderful. I think someone as beautiful as you should perform grander moves, though."

The princess smiled incandescently. "Please explain."

"I'll do you one better. I'll show you." Derrick's tone exuded competence.

He restarted the music, allowing it to fill the room and relax the atmosphere. Misty attempted to focus on him at the same time as she readied her body to begin dancing when the music commenced. With a few twists, turns, and jumps, the prince glided from one side of the room to the other, moving with more poise than she had known any man could have, leaving her speechless.

"Wow," she breathed as he turned to face her when his routine reached its conclusion. "You're amazing."

"Nah. I've just had tons of practice," he deflected, shutting off the music.

The interruption in the music trapped Misty mid-turn and she nearly lost her footing. For an instant, she worried that he'd noticed her sudden halt, but, luckily, he was too preoccupied with her eyes to care about what was going on with her feet.

"That jump-kick thing you did at the very end seemed pretty complicated," she enthused as he continued to gaze at her. "Does it have a name? Or was it a premiere creation that'll be christened at a later date?"

Her banter had no effect on Derrick, whose eyes stayed locked on her face.

"Hello?" she laughed, barreling on when he didn't respond. "That step, what's it called? You landed one earlier too." She nervously twirled her hair around a finger.

"Oh, sorry," Derrick apologized, finally stunned back into reality. "It's a grand jetè. Would you like me to show you how it's done?"

"Sure," Misty acquiesced, shifting to burn some of the energy that had her on edge. "That would be great."

"Okay, so. Your arms are where everything starts," he coached. "You can have them in fourth position, with one above your head and the other extended out and rounded like this." He demonstrated the pose in a simple yet flawless manner. "There's also fifth position, where you have both of them above your head and slightly curved." Here, he transitioned fluidly. "But... I find that first position feels most natural when you're performing a grand jetè, where you have your arms out in front of you and rounded because that makes it easier to go into third position arabesque at the end of the jump. Arabesque techniques are used in ballet positions which require standing on one leg and moving another."

The princess was suddenly swept away by the passion Derrick had when he spoke about dance. *I wonder if I'll ever feel as passionate about something as he does about dance.* It was in that moment that she realized that having her wish come true was what she was just as passionate about. Knowing this, she willed herself to listen very carefully and make it happen as he continued. "Third position arabesque is where you have both arms extended out in front of your body with the arm on the same side as your supporting foot up slightly higher than the other like so," he once again demonstrated with flawless ease. A moment later he flashed her a grin. "You're up." Stepping back and a few feet to one side, he gave her space to work.

The wary smile Misty shot him was more a grimace than anything else. She loved Derrick's passion for dance, she did, but it also made her incredibly nervous. Although she had caught some of the knowledge he'd imparted, she wasn't looking forward to putting it into practice already. The way his body moved on instinct alone left her breathless and made it difficult to think coherently. Not wanting to let him in on this, she brought herself to her full height and set her limbs in first position.

His features went soft as he assessed her posture. "Beautiful. Bring your arms down just a bit, if you can," he instructed, repositioning them himself before she could. "When you extend your arms, make sure that they're right in front of your belly button. That way they're not too high or too low. It's also best to put your arms straight out and go into the arabesque position I mentioned before so that they are relaxed when you go airborne because it's actually dangerous to be off the ground while your arm is rounded due to the tension you have to have in your arms to properly hold the position," he explained. "You'd also be less likely to catch yourself if you fall with your arms rounded," he added, almost as an afterthought.

Now it was the princess's turn to gape. "Who said anything about falling?" she asked, worry suddenly evident in her voice.

The prince placed a hand on her shoulder and squeezed it softly. "Don't worry. I'll never let that happen," he assured her. "I'll always be here to catch you."

After a quiet 'thank you,' escaped her lips the prince nodded and continued. "It also has to do with technique. Many dancers don't like to have their arms rounded while in airborne positions or using arabesque techniques because it tends to make their arms look droopy."

The princess chuckled. "You sure know a lot about this."

"What can I say? I take my hobbies seriously." He shrugged nonchalantly, one side of his mouth lifting into the beginning of a smile. "Now, let's try to get your legs right. You're going to need one to be out in front of you and the other behind you. Like so." He modeled the words, providing her with a visual in addition to his audio.

"Good?" she asked, mimicking his motions.

He glanced over and nodded. "That's great. Remember to point your toes, though. You're going to want to have your legs as in as much of a line as possible."

Misty stretched her legs farther, grateful she had the music in the background to concentrate on. "Is this better?"

Derrick evaluated her stance. "Yep, you've got it. If you try loosening up, your steps wouldn't be as forced. You're too wrapped up in the completion; exceptional dancing incorporates a large amount of artistry into the process," he counseled.

Taking a deep, cleansing breath, the princess shook her body to get rid of some of the tension that had built up over the last few days; she then took a second shot at the appropriate stance in hopes of impressing him.

"Perfect!" Derrick congratulated excitedly before, "You ready to break out the big gun?"

Misty bit her lip anxiously. "I don't know," she admitted, hiding her trembling hands behind her.

"You are, trust me. You'll be fine. I'll break it down for you," he coaxed. "How about starting with another chassé to ease yourself into it?"

She agreed, pleased that he'd paid attention during her impromptu ballet sequence; she leapt up then, holding her frame motionless above the floor for a breath before reaching outward smoothly and composedly as she found her feet again. She landed in first position, her heels together and her toes perfectly pointed out. Without even thinking about it, she spread her heels apart into second position, gliding her left foot in front of her right foot repeatedly as though her feet were chasing one another, performing a flawless chassé

"Nice," Derrick encouraged, smiling from ear to ear.

I should add a demi-plié this time to really impress him, Misty flashed him a smile as she moved her feet back into first position.

Taking a deep breath she performed another chassè, bending her knees with her toes still pointed out, forming an immaculate demi-plié as she once again glided her right foot in front of her left foot. "Great. Building on that, your front leg needs to bend at the knee, and then straighten. Like before," he pointed out, making it seem like the simplest thing she'd ever do.

Misty was astonished to find that the combination turned out to be fairly uncomplicated.

Derrick's excitement grew stronger. "Perfect. You're a natural! You're definitely ready for more. Next perform a dèveloppè. Simply take your supporting foot, brush it back, and bring it out, like you're kicking something. Then leap up and forward, eventually landing on your other foot."

"Easy as pie," she bit out sarcastically.

"Chin up, beautiful. It's all you," he assured her. "Remember. Focus only on the music."

His support enabled the princess to carry out the steps perfectly.

"You're amazing!" he cheered when this was finished. "Now, put all the moves together and you've got yourself a grand jeté." His positivity was infectious.

"Says the man who has been doing them his whole life," Misty laughed softly.

"C'mon. All that's left to do is put all the pieces you've done together. You won't even break a sweat." He punctuated this with a wink.

The gesture melted the last of her hesitation and she firmly resolved to do her best and accept whatever the results were. Taking a deep breath, she followed through with this plan, praying that her technique was solid enough to impress Derrick.

"Exquisite," he praised, obviously a bit stunned by the outcome. "I can't believe you caught on so quickly. I'm impressed."

Pleasure and gratitude were written in the princess's eyes as she turned the approval around. "Yeah, well, I had a great teacher—"

The prince interjected, "—who needs some sunlight. Fresh air, my lady?" he offered, holding out his arm to her.

"Sure," she accepted eagerly, locking their arms together so they could head outside.

"This is beautiful!" Misty exclaimed on several occasions as she and the prince strolled through the castle grounds, continuing their wonderful period of getting to know one another.

"Thank you. Honestly, I think the beauty of this place is somewhat lost on me," he confessed in an undertone.

She blinked, pausing their progress and turning toward him in disbelief. "How is that possible?"

Derrick's lips quirked sheepishly. "Growing up here desensitized me. I don't know anything else; therefore, the grandeur of my home means very little, as I have nothing to hold it against in comparison. Other than times like these when I have the chance to take it all in through new eyes, that is," he amended.

"You're lucky to have grown up here," Misty remarked, unable to stop her voice from taking on a wistful quality.

"I'm sure that where you grew up is equally idyllic," the prince assured softly.

"My home may be beautiful, but I haven't spent much time outside of its walls. This walk is much more preferable than any day spent there." The happiness she felt at the truth of this statement bled into her voice.

"Glad to hear it," Derrick said, his tone just as upbeat as hers. "If you like the outdoors this much, why haven't you spent more time there?"

"Well, my par—," she began, cutting herself off when she saw the blue and purple butterfly that had settled on her shoulder.

"Oh, look! Its colors are so vivid." The princess kept her volume low so as not to disturb the insect. "I love butterflies," she expanded for Derrick's benefit as she kept a watchful eye on her new winged friend.

The prince could only stare in wonder as Misty closely examined the butterfly before guiding it onto her finger, carefully lifting it, and looking on in satisfied fascination as it flew away. Derrick couldn't believe how quickly he'd been entranced by the woman in front of him. While the prince loved the way her eyes lit up like sparklers whenever she was animated about something and how, when he was beside her, he could detect the faintest hint of lavender in her chestnut brown hair, her truly compassionate personality sealed the deal for him. *I've never met a sweeter, gentler, or more beautiful woman in my life*, he thought to himself; this directed him toward the fact that he needed to do everything in his power to show her the depth of his love for her and ensure that she would remain always at his side.

As this idea occurred to him, he pulled her closer and suggested, "Let's get back to dancing."

Misty's entire body hummed with more fatigue and soreness than she'd ever experienced, but she didn't want to admit that and disappoint him. Instead, she dragged herself, as optimistically as she could, into position; Derrick's arms circling her waist as he shook his head and drew her into a hug was not the evolution of this scenario that she'd expected.

The two swayed together in companionable silence for a while before Derrick established enough space between them to make steady, meaningful eye contact with her. Buoyancy bloomed in her chest, leaving her floating on cloud nine. Her assumption that he would kiss her fizzled when he fixed a puzzled glance on her chest. "Your necklace looks different today."

The observation made Misty crash back to reality and she shot the prince a look that echoed the feeling. "What?"

"Your necklace is different today," he repeated, gently lifting the chain closer and examining it. "I wouldn't have thought to put opals in it, but I like them."

Nausea suddenly hit Misty as she was reminded of the specifics that the magic of the last two days had allowed her to forget about. "I'm a little tired all of a sudden," she lied.

Her admission elicited a fleeting frown from Derrick. "Of course. It's getting late. You and Dex should stay another night."

"Thank you." An objection was out of the question with the third stone of her necklace as close to turning into an opal as it was. Misty's time was running out.

Chapter Five

The second night Misty passed in the castle's beautiful canopy bed did not prove nearly as restful as the first. She tossed and turned for most of the night, debating whether the bond she felt between herself and Derrick was real. Had he truly fallen for her, or was he being courteous out of royal duty? If he had genuine feelings for her, would he kiss her and own up to them by day's end, or would he continue being guarded? What would happen to her, her family, and Starryton if he didn't love her? These questions haunted her as she fought, in vain, to devise a plan that would guarantee her the prince's kiss and unwavering, irrevocable love before it was too late.

Waking far too early the next morning, the princess decided she was too tired and sore to face down a leotard again and, instead, settled on a red dress tight enough not to impede her movements, but still tasteful, so she could avoid having Derrick's mind wander. She expected this day to be much like the one before it and she hoped to have time to further develop her plan as they danced. As it turned out, this was not meant to be. This became evident when the prince knocked on her door as she finished preparing for the day.

"Oh, good. You're ready. Come with me. I have the entire day planned," Derrick clutched her hand in his then, as a thought struck him, relaxed his grip. "That is, if you wish to, of course." He brushed a hand through his hair restlessly.

"I wouldn't have it any other way," Misty promised, perking up a bit at the prospect of an excursion.

"Well then, your chariot awaits, my princess."

Misty's insides somersaulted at his choice of words. He had treated her like royalty from the moment he'd saved her from meeting a tragic demise even though he knew nothing of her noble rank. This was only one of the countless reasons why she loved him, even if it did somewhat outweigh the others.

The princess found it difficult to contain her delight the moment she and Derrick approached the horse-drawn carriage waiting for them in the expansive outdoor entryway. She had seen similar carriages before, often dreaming of taking a ride in one. This hope was forever being dashed by her parents' ongoing fear. She raced ahead of Derrick, ascending into the carriage with bliss suffusing every part of her being. She was fully aware that this might be her only chance to fulfill this fantasy and she intended to make the most of it.

Misty and Derrick toured the kingdom, politely acknowledging passersby as he introduced her to all of Mooncrest's landmarks, from the library to Kingdom Hall.

"I'd kill for some pasta right now. You hungry?" the prince asked, the query having been triggered by a quiet little bistro coming into view as they rounded a corner.

"I could eat," she laughed, squeezing his hand a little as he handed her down from the carriage.

"I was hoping you'd say that." He placed a hand on the small of her back, ushering her inside.

Misty held in a gasp as she took in the bistro around her. The intricately painted murals on the walls and small bushels of grapes hanging from the ceiling transported her to Italy within seconds. She was ecstatic to see that they had the whole restaurant, and its enormous pasta buffet, to themselves.

"Did you arrange this?" she marveled, her eyes going wide as they lit on new aspects of her surroundings.

"Hey, I'm a busy guy. I can't cook all of our meals, but I can make sure we always enjoy them." His smile as he proclaimed this made her knees liquefy.

"It's wonderful! Everything you've done since I met you is!" she swiveled to tell him, pausing in the midst of filling her plate to the brim with cheese-smothered ziti.

"You, darling, are the one who's wonderful. This required nothing but some creative thinking," he countered sincerely, taking a cue from her as to his entree before pointing her to a candlelit table in the back of the room with his breadstick.

"I have another surprise for you," Derrick hinted as they finished their quiet, romantic lunch.

"Another?" Misty asked around her last bite. "What did I do to deserve such excellent treatment, if I may inquire? she grinned.

"You're a beautiful dancer, you know."

It took her a minute to process the rapid shift in subject but, once she did, she managed a heartfelt 'thank you'. Then her face fell as it dawned on her that her ability to dance beautifully might not be a reality much longer.

"Where'd that brilliant smile go? It's time for dessert." Derrick's voice pleaded with her to join in his fun again; now that he'd gotten a taste of partnership, he was loath to let it slip away.

Misty focused her attention on the prince, then the buffet table, before returning it to him. "I don't see any desserts," she whispered conspiratorially, her brows furrowing in confusion.

The prince's lips lifted upward at the corners. "Come with me."

"What? Where are we go—?" Misty's sentence trailed off, unfinished, as he led her out the door, down a couple of streets, and into a chocolate shop.

"Pick your favorite, my lady," he said sweetly, moving a demonstrative hand under one of the vast shelves that held an assortment of confectionary delights.

"You pick for me and I'll pick for you," she suggested excitedly, her face brimming with mischief.

"I like how you think."

Misty was thrilled to find that Derrick had selected an array of miniature homemade peanut butter cups for her. The dark chocolate cashews she passed to him got an equally positive review.

"How did you know these were my favorite?" he asked, holding the bag up, unnecessarily, as a visual.

"You seem like a dark, nutty guy. What can I say?" she got all of this out without taking in additional air, ending with an innocent shrug and a tide of sing-songy laughter that gave her a momentary stomachache.

"Hey!" he hit her playfully, feigning shock and outrage. "I'm not sure how I should take that."

She shook her head to clear it with a "don't worry. I'm partial to nutty things" that cracked in the middle as her voice thinned.

"That's a weight off my mind," he exhaled, wiping the non-existent sweat of his forehead with a palm. "By the way, do you mind if we make one more stop before we head back to the castle?" he segued, munching on the last of his candy.

"Of course not," she declared. "Where to, sir?"

Derrick's demeanor became self-deprecating in the blink of an eye. "The antique store. My mother loves teapots more than she loves orchids, if you can believe it. I want to see if any of their new acquisitions will work with her collection. I'm in need of a birthday gift for her."

"Oh." Misty hesitated, scrutinizing her feet like they were the most interesting things in the world. She was uncertain, first, about meeting his parents and then, to an even greater degree, by the idea that he may not want her to.

Placing his hands on her shoulders in an attempt to calm worries he knew nothing of but could sense nonetheless, he squeezed them gently. "Don't worry! The castle will be your respite for as long as you like. I'd love for you to accompany me to the celebration we're having, actually."

Meeting his gaze, Misty let out a breath she didn't know she'd been holding, her words pillowed on the puff of air. "I wouldn't miss it!" she wrapped her arms around his shoulders, giving him a quick hug as he held the door for her.

Catching up to her with one long stride, he laced their fingers together and they went into the antique shop across the street. She found herself transfixed by how perfectly their hands fit with one another.

As they came face to face with endless aisles of wares, he let go of her hand, floundering in picking a path for them to take. Finally, he decided, "Kitchenware is usually towards the back. I'm going to investigate. Go wherever the wind blows you," he advised sagely, shooting her a wink before he started his search.

Misty giggled. "I'll remember that," she called after him, amid thoughts that this was her first experience in an actual store; her personal shopper and stylist had always come to her tower. The fact that the merchandise here had been around for longer than her grandparents had been alive was just an added bonus. Keeping this in mind, she perused the items cautiously, admiring each equally, from a big antique armoire to a small bumblebee paperweight.

She stopped in her tracks when she spotted a small box carved out of wood and trimmed in gold; as a finishing touch, it had a trio of painted butterflies on top. The princess picked up the box with care, cradling it as though its adornment had come to life. Lifting the lid carefully, she was delighted to discover that it wasn't a simple box, but, rather, a musical one complete with a tiny spinning ballerina in a purple tutu; her fairy wings intricately painted to match the brush-stroked butterflies. Her face exploded in unabashed pleasure as her ears registered the song from *A Midsummer Night's Dream* she'd danced to the day before.

"Whatchya got there?" Derrick asked as he wandered up behind her.

Misty jumped, startled by the sound. "Oh, nothing. A music box." She shut the box, carefully put it back on its shelf, and spun around. "Did you find anything?"

The prince grinned in satisfaction. "Yep, I hit the jackpot. Look at this!" he held out a porcelain teapot with a purple orchid painted on the side, urging her to look at it more closely.

"Oh, it's beautiful! Your mother's going to love it," she gushed, turning it in her hands so that she could get a look at each side.

"Glad we agree." The prince moved to stand at the register. "Sir, we'll take this," he placed the teapot on the counter, "as well as the music box the lady was admiring."

Misty shook her head in protest. "Oh, no. No. That's too mu—"

Derrick put a finger against her lips to cut her off. "I insist," he bent forward to tell her. "If you'd seen your face when you were looking at it, you wouldn't be fighting me. It's more than a music box to you."

Knowing she couldn't deny this assertion, the princess allowed him to pay, kissing him on the cheek in gratitude as they departed. "Thank you so much."

His cheeks pinked lightly at the attention. "You're welcome, beautiful. Keep it safe, okay? You never know when life will require a little music."

"Definitely," she agreed, accepting the intricate square from him and gently placing it in her handbag which she was thankful to have brought with her that day as well as on the entire adventure.

With that completed, they returned to the carriage arm in arm.

"I have one more trick up my sleeve," Derrick admitted, the castle grounds becoming visible over the next rise.

"I'm beginning to not detest surprises, which is definitely a first," she gasped laughingly.

"Wow. I'm touched." He placed a hand over his heart, playing the part of a man astounded by emotion. Guiding her descent onto solid ground as he spoke, he continued, "There's a section of the castle you haven't seen yet." Here, he placed a gentle hand over her eyes and proceeded to walk her to the edge of the property.

The princess had had every intention of making some kind of cute observation when they began to make their way across the grass, but the feeling of his hand on her skin ended up overriding everything else.

A moment later, he brought her to a stop and whispered: "You ready, beautiful?" into her hair.

She shuddered, though not in repulsion, as his breath ghosted over her. "As I'll ever be."

Taking his hand away, he let her assess her surroundings: a greenhouse that also happened to be a butterfly garden.

Stepping through its door left Misty in the confines of a magical world. Hundreds of beautiful, vibrant butterflies fluttered around her, trying to decide which of the tropical flowers that littered their habitat was best to land on. An underlying floral fragrance added another layer of beauty to the environment as these were blended with the sound of trickling water emanating from a stream in the center of the building. The princess looked at Derrick, felt her stomach quivering, and laughed as she wondered if there were as many butterflies fluttering around in it as there were in the greenhouse.

"This is amazing," she breathed, turning in circles to take in all of the available sights.

"I had a feeling you'd like it." He nodded in confirmation. "This became my mother's new baby after my sister left the nest but, now that she isn't home as much as in years past, she's entrusted me with its upkeep."

"I envy you. I'd love to nurture a place like this," Misty expanded wistfully.

"Maybe you should." Derrick's voice was quiet, filled with doubt.

"What?" the princess shifted her attention away from the butterflies and toward the prince, blinking at him in confusion.

He reached out to her, eliminating the space between them. "Misty." He paused then, gathering himself before soldiering on. "I brought you here because I thought it was the perfect place to tell you I—"

Misty's breath caught in her throat—she couldn't help hoping to hear the words she'd wanted to hear, if she was being honest, from the minute she'd met him. These never made it out though; the next thing she knew, there was a knock on the door.

The prince sighed and gently released her, holding up a finger. "Hold that thought."

No sooner had Derrick opened the door than a nervous, pudgy older man with salt and pepper hair and a thin mustache nearly fell through it.

"Bernie, what're you doing here?" he swiveled around to elucidate, "Misty, my butler, Bernie. He's supposed to be *away* this weekend," the prince clarified, putting emphasis on his preferred location.

"My apologies, your majesty, but it seemed pertinent that I intrude. Trovella has procured a cache of crown jewels and has taken to manifesting the citizens' of Mooncrest deepest nightmares."

The prince's eyes widened and he hastily turned, putting a hand to Misty's cheek and stroking it. "I have to go. Stay in the castle with Dex and Cliff. You'll be safe with them."

He turned and went out before Misty could object. She wanted to respect his wishes, really she did, but she couldn't keep still and soon ran to catch up with him.

Chapter Six

Terror washed over Misty as soon as she stepped off the castle grounds. Thunder crashed in the ink-black sky as bats flapped their wings so fast that the wind became like ice. Ghostly figures also moved there, leaving a fog in their wake that was too thick to let her see two feet ahead. Her palms sweating despite the bitter cold, the princess's pulse quickened and her heart lodged in her throat. Unlike most of the subjects surrounding her, who seemed to be under the impression that screaming would somehow save their lives, she kept her fear to herself. That is, until she felt a twitch on her leg, finding a tarantula when she investigated. Then all bets were off. This was even truer when she realized that a multitude of its kind had decided to add their sinister pitter-patter to the symphony of horrifying sounds already surrounding her. Kicking to get the arachnid off her leg, Misty stopped screaming long enough to sob; she had caused this nightmare. After exhausting all of her emotion, she contemplated the safest, quickest way to traverse the demon-plagued darkness that lay between her and Trovella.

The princess had difficulty locating a path through the gloom, until Dex charged toward her through the thick cloud cover, Cliff clinging to his back. She almost sent them back to where they'd come from, but she thought better of it before the order could roll off her tongue. While she would never forgive herself if anything happened to either of them, she also was in dire need of their support. After Cliff perched on her shoulder, she let Dex lead the three of them into the woods. The dog's sense of direction proved exemplary; in no time, the small group had arrived at Trovella's hut where Misty encountered a sight more terrifying than all of the apparitions she'd seen tonight combined. Biting her tongue to keep her shriek at bay, she struggled to compose herself in the face of the image in front of her. The troll stood outside of her hut, snarling with unrestrained malice as she held a tarantula-covered Prince Derrick firmly in her grasp.

"Let him go! This is my battle, not his," Misty proclaimed forcefully, pushing past the fact that her heart was making a valiant effort to break free of her chest. Her command was loud enough to startle Trovella and make her loosen her hold on the prince.

"I've been expecting you, dear child," bellowed the troll, scowling hungrily at the princess.

Trovella's distraction gave Derrick a window to pry himself out of her hand, scattering his coat of spiders as he moved. When he hit solid ground, he made a run for Misty.

"What are you doing here?" His question had an urgent edge to it and he stroked her cheek with great concern. "What does she mean, she's 'been expecting you'?"

The princess's panic over cluing Derrick in to the whole truth consumed her so completely that the bats beginning to swarm around them didn't even register. She gathered every ounce of courage she had left in her, blew out a centering rush of air, and faced him. "I gave Trovella access to the crown jewels." Her voice wavered and she caught her lower lip between her teeth in an attempt to regain control.

A mixture of confusion and concern washed over Derrick's features. He opened his mouth to reply, but was cut off as Trovella lumbered toward them.

"I'll explain everything later," she rushed. "Please go check on Dex and Cliff."

"Get the crown. We can fix this if we get the crown," he advised urgently, enveloping her in a farewell embrace. She relaxed into him for a few seconds and, when they broke apart, she stood with Trovella looming above her while Derrick ran to fulfill her earlier request.

"Fortunately for me, you're too late," Trovella bit out once they were alone. In the next instant, she let out a roar of a laugh as the sky above them turned from black to blue and the sun began to retreat into the horizon. A shiver coursed through Misty's body as she glanced from Trovella to the sun and back again.

"That's right, Princess. Your wish is about to expire and your precious little kingdom, as well as Derrick's, will be mine," Trovella all but screamed her threat, bending down until her gruesome face was only an inch from Misty's.

"We'll see about that," Misty boasted, trying to exude confidence in spite of the fact that she felt very little running through her. Trovella would never willingly part with the crown, so the princess devised a method of using the troll's weapons against her. "You don't scare me. Earthquakes do, though. Start an earthquake right now and I'll end this night quivering in a corner, begging for help. I swear. Nothing really matters, anyway," she taunted the troll.

Trovella scoffed haughtily, her eyes narrowing in annoyance. "Of course it does. You're only saying it doesn't because I have the crown."

Misty shook her head in denial. "That thing is nothing more than a useless hunk of metal."

As Misty spoke, Trovella stared at her, growing more enraged with each second that passed. "Dear child, there's magic in it. Powerful magic. Magic strong enough to grant me kingdoms that don't belong to me."

"You might have magic, but you have no real power. The power I possess is strong because I have a heart. You, however, probably have coal, black as night, where your heart should be!" Misty shouted, trying to keep her adrenaline flowing as the ground beneath her started to quiver. Although Trovella had indeed fallen into Misty's trap, the myriad of ways that her earthquake brainstorm could backfire terrified the princess. She was running out of time and had to act fast, so she yanked her music box from her handbag, opened it, and began to dance as soon as it played.

"I don't need a heart when I have royal crown jewels," Trovella gritted out loudly over the noise of the music and the splitting earth beneath her.

The princess rolled her eyes as she continued to move her limbs succinctly. "Weren't you listening to anything I just said? My heart, as well as the pride and love it contains for those closest to me, is what makes that…" she flung an arm in the direction of the item Trovella was clutching, "…so special. Nothing else."

"You and Princey don't know what pride is!" Trovella's exclamation had the chasm in the ground yawning wider within seconds. "It wouldn't have been as sinfully simple to sabotage that idiotic cooking competition if your families had had pride." An evil laugh rolled out of the troll before she went on, her mouth remaining set in a grim line.

"Crown jewels or not, I am the fiercest being to ever grace this land!" Trovella's eyes became bright red as her anger reached its peak and the fault in earth stretched even further.

Still twirling to her music box, Misty's eyes widened as this occurred, and she jumped from the land on the thinner side of the crack to the land on the other, more expansive side. As she found her feet again, she recalled Trovella's revelation that she'd been responsible for the feud between the two families, and fury took over. Truth be told: she'd never been as angry as she was at present in her entire life. Not dwelling on the decision for very long, she took drastic measures. "Prove you don't need the jewels. Give me the crown back," Misty pleaded, continuing to dance.

Trovella scoffed in derisive amusement at the princess. "Dear child, I'm afraid that's never going to happen."

Misty assessed the landscape behind her and saw that the sun was much closer to setting than it had been ten minutes before, at the beginning of this confrontation. This knowledge influenced her next retort. "Why not? The sun has all but set. My wish has almost dissolved. What have you—"

Suddenly, Dex flashed in front of Misty, with Cliff attached securely to the fur on his back and Derrick sprinting at his side. Before she could get any words out, Cliff, snatched the crown off Trovella's head and brought it to rest above Derrick's. The added weight of Derrick and the animals as well as the current commotion split the cracked surface of the earth into a more prominent fissure. During this, Misty concentrated only on her footwork. As long as her music box was still functioning, she would keep dancing. She hated not being able to help, but the only way to keep from falling through the crack in the ground, encroaching on her further with every second, was to dance. She watched apprehensively as the scene before her unfolded, finding a small amount of comfort in the fact that Dex and Cliff would not shrink away from this fight.

"Oh, you little…" Trovella began as Dex backed out of her reach and Cliff brought the crown further into the air above Derrick, taunting her and making her lean forward toward it.

Eyes darting from one side of the nearby chasm to the other, the princess allowed herself the luxury of believing that this chaos would end once the sun had fully set. This might mean that their kingdoms would cease to exist, but at least they wouldn't be horribly manipulated first. Her musings were cut short when Trovella made another grab for the crown, taking a step forward this time in lieu of bending her body to lean in.

Misty smiled to herself, dancing and locking eyes with Trovella as the troll tripped into the now continuously expanding break in the ground. When this happened, the princess saw a window of opportunity and took it. Without considering the consequences, she spun until she'd gotten behind Trovella, who was struggling to find her balance after her tumble. From this position, Misty executed a grand jetè just as Derrick had taught her to, landing a blow to the troll's tailbone as she came out of it. A piercing scream escaped from Trovella's lips as she fell face first into the abyss in front of them, her arm still extended towards the crown as she plummeted into the darkness; the tarantulas, bats, ghostly figures, and all of the other ghoulish creatures that had made an appearance this evening trailed after her, until everything was swallowed by the crack and the ground knit itself together over the mess. As the sun finally fully descended, plunging the world into night, Misty's knees buckled and she collapsed. Derrick rushed over, cradling her in his arms and brushing his fingers over most of her body, ensuring she was still intact. "Listen. I know you just saved us and everything," he began, laughing. "But you've got some explaining to do, beautiful."

"I—I—I didn't know." Misty's voice trembled, tears filling her eyes.

"What didn't you know?" Derrick asked as gently as he could.

What followed was the princess's confession of her royal status in Starryton, her disability, her discovery of the history between their families, and her wish, to the prince.

When Misty finished her account, the prince laughed again, affectionately, and held her against him. She shook her head, not understanding what she was seeing. "It's not funny, Derrick. Both of our kingdoms were just nearly destroyed and now I've reverted to my plain, sheltered self. All that's left is for me to go back to my tower," she hiccupped as she started to sob.

"Don't cry," Derrick soothed, using his sleeve to wipe away her tears. "You're far from plain and you're not going anywhere, unless it's home with me."

Misty's brows furrowed as she looked up at him. Her 'What?' came out in a whisper.

Derrick's face broke into a smile a second before he let out a low whistle. Dex and Cliff, neither of whose absence Misty had noted, approached them dragging her wheelchair on a rope between them.

"When Trovella disappeared this showed up in her place. The critters here insisted on bringing it to you," Derrick informed her kindly as he assisted her in transferring into the machine.

The princess hung her head, shame suffusing her being. "I'm sorry about everything. I just couldn't imagine a wonderful dancer like you wanting to spend time with someone like me. I have no coordination," she confessed.

"Look at me," Derrick insisted, his canine and aviary assistants observing the interaction between him and Misty from a few yards away.

Misty acquiesced to his request, reluctantly raising her eyes to meet his.

"I never liked you only for your body or your ability to dance. I like—er—love—you, because you're compassionate and beautiful, and because you've brought more fun into my life in three days than I've had in my twenty-three years." Derrick's expression seesawed between contentment and uncertainty as he waited for her to respond.

The princess was stunned. "Wait. You—What?"

"I love you," he repeated with startling clarity. "If you had come to my castle in your wheelchair, I would still have fallen for you because your personality is unparalleled. Plus, the scent of lavender always accompanies you. How can I give that up?" he shrugged, permitting himself a small, good-natured chuckle, but he sobered when he saw that she was still upset.

"No. I'm not any of those wonderful adjectives," Misty blubbered, shaking her head emphatically. "I'm selfish, so I didn't listen to my parents. All of this was about the things that I wanted; I wasn't thinking about anyone else. I'm responsible for every bit of tonight's awfulness. I'm a horrible person."

"Please don't cry. You have it all wrong," the prince murmured, wrapping her in his arms again. "You're amazing, beautiful, smart, and brave."

Misty's forehead wrinkled in consternation. "Brave? I'm definitely not brave."

Derrick's eyes widened. "Yes." He ducked his head, locking his gaze with hers. "You are. You had enough confidence in yourself not only to believe in happiness, but to also go after it. Not many people can say that. Besides, who says you can't dance?" Derrick grinned mischievously, maneuvering her wheelchair controller so that it twirled her in an arcing, dizzying circle.

Misty smiled brightly. "I love you."

Derrick beamed at her words, took her face between his hands, and kissed her. When they broke apart, he effused, "I love you too, beautiful. I love you just the way you are and can't imagine having a better partner as I make my preparations to reign."

Misty felt her features come together in imitation of his. "I love you, Derrick, but I don't think I should help you. My parents have always been under the impression that someone with my struggles can never lead an entire kingdom of people. I've heard it for long enough that it's hard for me not to accept it as truth," she admitted solemnly.

"I love you and I need you by my side," he assured. "Please stay in Mooncrest with me. I'll take care of everything else."

Misty picked at the hem of her dress, collecting her thoughts before looking up to deliver them. "I wish it were that easy, Derrick, but it's not. Our families' history and my disability are very real obstacles. Are we just supposed to ignore them?"

The prince shook his head, calmly insisting, "Everything will work out. All you have to do is trust that our love is strong enough to overcome anything and everything we may face in our future." He took her hand, squeezing it encouragingly.

Misty's fingers returned the pressure. "When you put it that way, how can I refuse?"

"You'll stay in Mooncrest with me then?" Derrick checked, keeping most of his exhilaration at bay.

The princess nodded, grinning from ear to ear. "I believe we're officially a couple," she confirmed. "Now, let's go home."

The prince rested his hands on her shoulders and attempted to turn his mood serious. "There is one thing I would like you to agree to before we leave, if you wouldn't mind."

"What's that?"

"Write your parents a letter telling them you're safe in Mooncrest."

Misty backed her chair away from him, giving herself space. "Derrick, I can't do that. They'll come after me in a heartbeat and drag me away from you." Her demeanor as she discussed the inevitability of this setback was matter-of-fact and somber.

Derrick slung a comforting arm around her. "If and when your parents come for you, we'll deal with them together, sweetheart. No one is going to take you anywhere you aren't willing to go," he vowed. "But it's still important that they know you're safe. If I were them, I'd want that much. "Do you understand where I'm coming from?" he inquired with much sincerity.

Misty was shocked to find that, in fact, she did. Knowing the necessity of the act wouldn't make it any easier to carry out. She dreaded having to compose the missive in large part because she had no idea what to say. The love she noted in Derrick's eyes gave her courage to at least attempt the feat, though.

"Okay," she sighed. "I'll get in touch with them."

"Thanks, sweetie. I'd join in, but I never know where to send correspondence when my parents travel." He waved a dismissive hand. "Anyway, I'm sure everything will work itself out."

With that, Derrick pressed his lips to her forehead, and led their little group home to the castle.

Chapter Seven

The next morning, Misty woke up in the tulip room rested, but surprised at having been greeted by a member of the prince's staff rather than Derrick himself.

"Hello, miss, I'm Marie. The prince has asked that I assist you with your morning activities." The petite brunette grinned warmly and extended her hand.

Shaking the proffered limb, Misty relaxed. "It's nice to meet you. Where is the prince this morning?"

Marie chuckled. "Don't worry, miss. You'll see him after a bit. Now, tell me, how do we go about enhancing your natural beauty?"

"Give me your hands, please," Misty requested, extending hers demonstratively. Marie grasped them gently. "Now, pull me into a sitting position and sling my feet over the edge of the bed."

Her kind assistant did as instructed.

Raising herself slowly, Misty used her hands for balance, took a few steps to the left, and came to a stop in front of her wheelchair. She sagged forward against the backrest gratefully, taking a breather from her exertion. "I'm going to have you put on my shoes now because that makes it easier to stand up when I'm getting my clothes on," she explained, motioning toward the items of discussion. Once her footwear was secured, Misty moved her feet underneath her and pushed herself up into her seat.

"Next comes my teeth," she announced.

After Marie had applied paste to Misty's brush and the dental cleaning was done, it was time to address her upper half. She regularly completed her routine in this order because her occasional spasms made it almost impossible to keep her outfits free of toothpaste stains.

"Please apply deodorant before helping me pull my dress over my head." Misty stretched her arms over her head as high as she could in order to simplify this process. Marie followed these directions to the letter before assisting Misty in standing a second time and arranging her dress. Within minutes, the two women were in front of the vanity and ready to style her hair. Though this would probably have sounded strange to most people, while Misty appreciated the miracle she'd received and wouldn't forget it for as long as she lived, she was more at ease during her routine this morning than she had been for the past few days because she didn't have to fight to get her body to move in ways it wasn't used to.

"How do you normally wear your hair, miss?" Marie asked.

"Up, in a tight bun, most of the time," she responded. "Have you ever styled someone's hair into a bun?"

"Can't say I have, miss, but I'll try my best. Maybe you can walk me through it?" Marie smiled. She couldn't have been a day over 35, but the tiny wrinkles around her mouth revealed that she'd already weathered many storms in her life.

Misty handed over two hair ties and a scrunchie from her bag. "Start by using one hair tie to fashion a ponytail, then put the ponytail through the scrunchie. After that, it's a matter of wrapping my hair around the fabric like it's a Jell-O mold and using a little of this to ensure that my hair stays in place," she explained after taking The Royal Treatment out of her bag.

Marie laughed. "You've told people how to do this a time or two, haven't you, miss?"

The princess grinned as Marie put the finishing touches on the updo she was creating and then generously applied the hairspray. "Only about half a million. You did very well."

Examining her hair in the mirror, Misty's lips quirked upward. It wasn't perfect, but she looked more regal and like herself than she had in quite a while. Although she would never enjoy having to have other people help her, she appreciated it more now that she'd spent some time without it.

Maybe this isn't so bad after all, she thought, with Marie in the background asking about the next step.

"Well, I usually put on makeup and jewelry, but I don't have any with me," Misty tittered under her breath as she remembered Trovella's necklace and fleetingly wished that it hadn't disappeared along with her, "so this will have to do. I should go find Derrick now. Thank you so much for your help," Misty acknowledged appreciatively, waiting for her transportation to click to life.

"No, no, I must urge you to delay a minute, miss," Marie implored.

The princess's brows wrinkled in confusion. "Why? …and feel free to call me Misty," she added as an afterthought.

Marie shuffled anxiously. "Well, you see, the prince suspected you would be lamenting your lack of accessories, so he has tasked me with showing you the queen's jewelry collection. If there's anything you wish to borrow, His Highness has given his wholehearted blessing. Oh, he's also scheduled you an appointment with the queen's makeup artist."

Marie's case of nerves transferred itself to Misty and she found herself suddenly filled with hesitation. "Oh, no. I couldn't possibly wear the queen's jewels. My own mother doesn't even let me wear hers."

"Nonsense," Marie dismissed, waving away Misty's negativity. "The pieces are too beautiful to sit in a dark room and never be worn. There's also the argument that it could all be yours one day, anyway," she went on under her breath, turning toward the door while she spoke.

"Huh?" Misty blurted from her stationary position.

Marie's cheeks flushed red at being found out. "Nothing, miss, nothing at all. Please come along now. If you won't do it for me, do it for the prince."

Letting out a resigned sigh, the princess grabbed her handbag and gave her reflection a final glance before hurrying after Marie.

"Where are we going?" Misty huffed, once they'd been walking for a while and it seemed as though they should have run out of castle to go through. "I thought I'd seen this place from top to bottom."

Marie laughed sympathetically, her cheeks displaying the effort she was putting into their brisk pace. "There are parts of it that not even the prince has ventured into. Keep up, darling. We're almost there."

Eventually, they came upon a tiny door at the very back of a castle corridor, with a keypad affixed to its front in lieu of a lock or handle. Misty watched, wide-eyed, as Marie punched in a code, after which the door slid open with a loud *swish*, staying that way just long enough for the ladies to sneak through.

"Wow!" the princess's eyes became as big as saucers as she took in her surroundings. "I thought this kind of magnificence only existed in movies," she whispered, fascinated, as Marie carefully opened drawers and compartments of the large armoire that the room housed. While Misty loved the royal jewels in Starryton, they had been passed down from generation to generation and, as such, were tremendously outdated. The armoire before her, on the other hand, was full of elegant sapphire earrings, white-gold diamond pendants, and breathtaking emerald and ruby bracelets. She gasped when she found that the top drawer held a collection of gorgeous tiaras with more sparkle and shine than any that she had ever worn. Within seconds, one adorned with diamonds and amethysts caught her eye.

"Wow! I love amethysts," Misty exclaimed, evaluating her selection from a better vantage point.

Marie's countenance exuded satisfaction as she carefully removed the tiara from its space and held it out for the princess to take. "Try it on," she coaxed. "It will pair wonderfully with your dress and handbag."

Misty shook her head but remained silent, the knitting of her brows the only clue to her inner turmoil. "I couldn't possibly. Something might happen to it."

"Don't be silly," Marie chided maternally. "One must wear jewelry in order for it to be admired. Besides, every piece in here is insured to high heaven." She placed the tiara on Misty's head slowly, and handed her the small mirror she kept in her apron.

The princess hesitantly brought the mirror up from her lap, assessing her appearance. "Very pretty," she decided.

Marie pouted at the perceived understatement. "More than pretty. You look fabulous, miss, but not yet as regal as you were meant to," she proclaimed a moment before delving back into the armoire to ferret out further riches.

Thumbing through the various compartments at lightning speed, she eventually emerged with a necklace and bracelet, as well as a pair of earrings, all comprised of sterling silver, diamonds, and amethyst, a combination which matched the procured headpiece perfectly. Immediately after these were found, the ecstatic maid put everything on Misty. "Stunningly majestic. Off to the make-up artist with you!"

"Can't we—"

Marie sighed fretfully, stopping Misty mid-question. "No, no. We must finish quickly. Come," she prodded.

The princess began to protest again, but Marie scurried out of the room, forcing Misty to trail after her if she wanted to be heard. The next thing she knew, she was in an entirely different location, one she'd never seen before, being shoved in front of a person she'd never met. Said person frantically began adjusting Misty's face within mere seconds of laying eyes on it.

Why on earth is she a make-up artist? The princess inwardly wondered as she took in the six-foot-tall, blue-eyed blond, with luminescent white teeth, standing before her. *She would look like a model even if she refused to wear makeup.*

"I'm Shelly. It's great to meet you, miss. I must say, you have terrific cheekbones. We need to accentuate them a bit, though. Smile for me?"

Misty heeded the request, hoping the makeup would help her look half as beautiful as the woman applying it.

"Will you walk me through the way you apply my makeup?" the princess asked. "I want to be able to tell my assistants how to recreate whatever look you're giving me."

Shelly put a hand to her chest, pretending to be pained. "You want me to tell you how to have someone else do my job?" she applied lavender eye shadow as she conversed.

Misty bit her lip, chagrined. "Well, I mean..."

Shelly laughed. "I was only playing, miss. I understand your motives and don't begrudge you. I'll have to tell you another day, though, because, right now, we must concentrate on readying you for your day with the prince," she said, applying mascara to Misty's lashes at the same time.

"That's all anyone is saying. It's starting to make me edgy," the princess admitted.

"Don't be," Shelly advised, patting her shoulder. "Presentation is half of the battle. You look great so you'll be great." She finished off Misty's look with light pink lipstick, before swiveling her towards the mirror so she could see it for herself.

Misty gasped as she took in her reflection. Although her assistants had always done a great job with her makeup, this was the first time she'd looked quite so imperial. *If only my parents could see me now*, she reasoned to herself as she turned back toward Shelly. "Thank you so much!"

The makeup artist gazed proudly at the princess for a minute, admiring her work. "You're most welcome, miss. You're beautiful. Don't worry about a thing. Go enjoy yourself."

"Thank you. I will!" the princess promised, heading off in search of Derrick.

* * *

As Misty sat down to breakfast in the dining room, she was surprised to find Derrick missing.

After several minutes had elapsed, Bernie entered the room. "What would you like to eat, my dear?"

"May I have chocolate chip waffles again, please?"

The older man considered her thoughtfully. "You may have anything you wish. I'll inform the kitchen staff immediately." With a courteous nod, he made his way in that direction.

Misty cleared her throat, getting his attention before he'd walked out of earshot.

The butler faced her again. "Yes, miss?"

"Before you go, do you happen to know where the prince is this morning?" she inquired nonchalantly.

Bernie grinned, amused. "I believe he is still in his bedchamber. Down the hall, to your left," he directed.

"Thanks. I'm going to say hello while the waffles are cooking." With that, she motored toward Derrick. Knocking lightly on his door, she paced in front of it as she waited for some form of acknowledgement.

"Come in," Derrick called faintly after a minute or so.

Slowly pushing the door open, Misty was mystified as to why Derrick was still in bed at this hour. Rushing to his side, she took his hand, unconsciously feeling for his pulse. "Holy...You're burning up!" she exclaimed, concern etched in the lines of her face.

He squeezed her hand lightly in reassurance. "I'll be okay," he breathed, a weak cough tumbling out. "I'm just not feeling very well today. You, on the other hand, look ravishing," he extolled, shooting her a half-hearted smile. The fact that it wasn't nearly as enthusiastic as others he'd given her over the past few days made her stomach drop.

"What can I do to help?" the princess asked, touching his cheek in concern. "Can I bring you medicine? Food? Cliff? Something else that's escaping me at the moment?"

Derrick turned all of this down with a shake of his head. "Thank you so much, beautiful. My staff already has a handle on all of that, though. Don't worry—it'll give you frown lines." He paused. "There is one thing I could really use help with, now that you mention it."

"Anything," Misty vowed, tightening her grip on his hand.

Studying her for a moment, Derrick finally feebly pronounced, "I really hope you mean that. Several citizens of Mooncrest requested an audience with me today, but I'm not in any condition to meet with them. Will you do it?" he exhaled the last part of his request on a coughing fit.

Misty dropped his hand with lightning speed. "Me? Why me? I couldn't possibly."

The prince reestablished the broken contact, adding some comforting pressure as he did so. "Yes, you can. You're royalty. You have to remember that."

She sighed resignedly. "Yes, but not here. Here, I'm pretty much a nobody."

"Nonsense!" Derrick denied emphatically. "You're somebody to me." After he'd gotten this out, his coughing worsened. Recovering himself after a few seconds, he continued, "I'd bet money that you've watched your parents conduct similar affairs and that you know *exactly* how to handle yourself."

'I hate how well he can read me, she thought, remembering numerous occasions that had transpired just as he'd described.

Having citizens request an audience with the royal family was a practice that had been used in her kingdom and, apparently, in Derrick's, for years. Such meetings were aimed at solving issues regarding wages, estates, and other volatile topics. Although Misty had seen her parents bring peaceful conclusions to the majority of the audiences they held, she wasn't convinced that she'd inherited any of their collective negotiation prowess. The more she turned the idea of attempting to have an audience with the people of Mooncrest over in her mind, the louder her father's words echoed in her mind: *You have a disability. You can't reign over a kingdom. It's not safe for you, or for the people.* As this loop went on, Misty could only look at the prince and cry. "I hate to disappoint you, but I really don't think I'm up for it," she whispered, her tears cascading downward.

Heaving himself up, the prince reached out and brushed her hair back behind her ear. "You are beautiful, kind, intelligent, and caring. I trust you. I know you can do this." He cupped her cheek as he reassured her. "I would never force you to do anything you feel uncomfortable with, though. If you're really opposed to it, I'll just cancel," he stated solemnly, brushing his lips against her forehead.

Derrick's forlorn tone conveyed his disappointment at the prospect of her not coming through for him; she bit her lip and made her decision. "I'll do it."

"I appreciate it so much. You look great, and you'll do great. Don't worry about anything. Explain that you're my trusted friend and everything after that will be smooth sailing." Here, he wrapped her in a warm, tight hug. *Even if this blows up in my face, at least I can put off writing that letter home,* she consoled herself; in her eyes, this was cowardice, but she had no way of changing her emotions about the situation.

After leaving Derrick to rest, Misty polished off her waffles before hesitantly heading out to meet his subjects who had already assembled.

Chapter Eight

With her heart pounding hard enough to pulse in her ears, Misty addressed the crowd before her. "Hello. I'm Misty Miles, a personal friend of Prince Derrick. Due to unforeseen circumstances, he is unavailable today, but has asked that I come and rectify your troubles as best I can." The princess avoided going into the finer details of Derrick's absence, so as not to induce panic. She projected a sunny demeanor, hoping she exuded enough confidence that no one would grill her too harshly about particulars.

After several moments with the people, Misty surmised that they were far too wrapped up in their own problems to be concerned with having to deal with someone new. No sooner had she finished her announcement than the yelling began. "Stop selling chocolate boxes. Candy is my niche," a thin, silver-haired gentleman yelled across the room, outrage distorting his features.

A gentleman close to his age, albeit heavier in stature, puffed out his chest defensively. "Pfft. Something that's your niche should approach perfection. Your candy comes nowhere close to this, and a little competition might do you some good."

"You'll never be real comp—"

Misty took a deep breath, praying that she could find a reasonable solution. Finally, she reprimanded the men before her. "Gentlemen. Gentlemen, please. I can't help you if you insist on carrying on in this way. Breathe, calm yourselves, and explain the source of your strife to me."

Misty heard her mother in the words she spoke, a sudden wave of longing hitting her at this realization. If her parents could see the actions she was currently taking, Misty wondered, what would their opinions be?

After following her command to the letter, the thin, silver-haired man began relaying his account, jolting her out of her reverie. "Miss, if I may, I am Maurice, the chocolatier of Mooncrest. This bozo to my left is Thomas, the kingdom's florist. He recently started selling chocolate boxes in his shop and it's cutting into my profits. What I'd like is for the royal family to order him to cease this practice."

Misty nodded in acknowledgement. "Thank you, Maurice. I would like to hear Thomas's side of things now."

The man in question beamed benevolently. "Of course, miss. The imbecile," he jabbed a finger in Maurice's direction, "to my right is correct. I started stocking candy in my shop because candy and flowers are a matched set. Obviously, the realm is in need of quality sweets because his are lacking." Thomas stopped, looking Misty straight in the eye for what followed. "Also, I would like to point out that, not long after I added this component to my business, Maurice started selling floral arrangements. Therefore, if I'm ordered to stop selling his wares, the same should be done with regard to him advertising mine."

Misty brought her hands together and laid them gracefully in her lap. "Well, gentleman, the answer to this dilemma appears to be fairly straightforward."

Both men gaped at her, each set of eyebrows knitted together in disbelief.

Misty smiled nervously, straightening her body in order to buy time to find the words to continue. "Well, as Thomas indicated, flowers and candy do go well together. With that said, I think the two of you should let bygones be bygones, close down your separate shops, and work together in a larger one that combines both of your areas of expertise."

"You want us to work together?" Maurice was wide-eyed, his shock evident as he drew frantic lines between himself and Thomas.

Misty pushed forward, undeterred. "Yes, I do. Some people aren't able to get up and go to work every day. You, gentlemen, should be grateful that you have this opportunity, as well as the fact that you've been blessed with the ability to do extremely well for yourselves in your respective fields. I expect that you'll find a way to work together and report your progress to me in a couple of weeks," she averred with authority.

Thomas moaned, eyeing Misty with disdain. Opening his mouth to express disapproval, he, instead, ended up doubled over, the result of Maurice aiming an elbow at his side.

The thinner man bobbed his head repeatedly and gave her a chastised smile. "You're absolutely right, miss. We're adults, adults who are going to build the greatest special occasion enterprise any realm has ever seen," he informed her matter-of-factly.

"That's what I like to hear." She dismissed both men with kindness and they made their way out quietly. Her face lit up when she saw that the next person in the queue was a little girl of no more than seven; she had clear blue eyes, strawberry-blond curls, and rosy cheeks. Incidentally, she also sat in a wheelchair.

"I'm Kara," the little girl started, exposing her deep dimples as she held out her hand.

"It's nice to meet you," Misty responded covering Kara's tiny hand with her own. "What can I do for you, sweetheart?"

"Well, I was gonna—" Kara chewed on the inside of her cheek, looking everywhere but ahead of her.

Misty cupped the child's shoulder gently. "You can tell me anything, sweetie. I'm here to help you," she coaxed.

"I was planning to make a wish and now I can't," the little girl admitted sadly, still biting her cheek.

This revelation sent Misty's head into a spin. She unconsciously copied Kara's eye movements from moments before, eventually gathering herself and returning to the issue at hand. "What were you going to wish for, and are your parents here with you? We should discuss this as a group." Her timbre remained calm in spite of her inner battle.

The little girl hung her head as tears welled in her eyes. "They didn't want me. No one wants me. My friends at Mooncrest Group Home are adopted every day, but I'm always left there." Wiping at the moisture on her face only prompted the girl to cry more profusely, but she persevered nonetheless. "It's because of this." Kara scowled at the wheels of her chair in frustration. "I was planning on finding Trovella and asking to walk and get adopted." Her speech was halting and broken as more tears spilled.

It took all of Misty's strength to stay composed in the face of this utter heartache. She launched into action in the only way she could think to. After deeming that all of the as-of-yet-unheard cases would be handled at a later date, she enveloped Kara in a hug that was strong enough to make the muscles in her arms burn before taking the young subject back to the group home with the intention of speaking with the staff.

* * *

"Oh, thank God!" a plump woman with curly gray hair, who looked to be around sixty, shouted as Kara and Misty walked through the group home's front door. "Where have you been? Everyone's been looking for you. You know better than to leave unattended!" the maternal woman shook a finger at her charge, fixing her with a stern glance.

Kara gnawed her bottom lip worriedly, staring at her shoes. "I'm sorry, Betsy," she mumbled. "I went to talk to the prince," she confessed shyly, her voice low and subdued.

Betsy sighed, her expression becoming softer with the release of air. "Kara, honey. How many times do I have to tell you to let go of the wishes? Nothing's going to happen—especially not now."

Misty, who'd been watching this exchange silently up until this point, coughed twice to remind them of her presence.

Kara smiled. "Betsy, this is Misty. She's Prince Derrick's friend and I met her today."

The princess chuckled and extended her hand to the older woman. "It's nice to meet you, Betsy," she acknowledged as the two of them shook to complete their acquaintance. "My apologies for the trouble. I thought it best that I bring Kara back myself. I hope this afternoon hasn't caused you too much stress."

"You have nothing to apologize for, miss," the older woman rushed, waving the words away and, at the same time, looking reproachfully at Kara again. "By the way, as Kara was kind enough to supply, I'm Betsy. I work as director and senior caretaker here at Mooncrest Group Home. Kara has had thorough training in our rules and will be punished for breaking them."

Misty nodded in understanding. "Yes, well. Before you get to that, do you mind if I talk to you in private for a moment?" she inquired sincerely.

"I can spare a minute," Betsy agreed. "My office is this way. Come with me." With that, she moved forward, motioning for the princess to keep pace with her, but turned back to Kara before they'd made it five yards. "Don't go anywhere, missy. We still have to discuss your punishment."

"Yes ma'am," the little girl breathed.

*　*　*

Betsy's office resided in the very back of the building. As Misty made the long trek to it, accompanied by the lady herself, she peered at her surroundings. Despite the fact that colorful pre-adolescent artwork featuring unicorns, kittens, fish, and various other animals, both real and fantastical, was displayed throughout the open, well-lit space, sadness permeated the air; it was as if each child in residence was fully aware that they may never have the chance to experience a parent's unconditional love. Although the princess wanted to help all of them, such a feat would never come to pass. Misty resolved to, regardless of everything else, keep an eye out for Kara. She had squashed the little girl's chance of speaking with Trovella, after all. As this light bulb went on in her brain, Misty came to the conclusion that she had to set out on a mission to find the solitary little girl a family.

"What did you want to talk about, miss?" Betsy queried, shutting the door of her office behind them.

"Kara," Misty told the older woman succinctly, with a polite smile and a serious tone. "I'm very concerned about her."

Betsy lowered herself into her desk chair contemplatively. "Am I correct in assuming that she told you the basis of her wish?"

"Yes, she filled me in on all of it."

The caring woman's head drooped a bit as she took a moment to massage her temples before circling her attention back to Misty. "I'm dreadfully sorry, miss. I've tried to dissuade her from the fact that walking will lead to finding a permanent home, but she refuses to listen," she elaborated. "Trovella being gone seems to have sent her into something of a tailspin due to the fact that, because of this, she's had to face the very last shred of her dream disintegrating." Betsy cleared her throat in an effort to maintain self-possessed. "You really shouldn't concern yourself about the child. I'll be sure to speak to her about this incident again but, as the saying goes, kids will be kids."

By the end of Betsy's soliloquy, Misty's heart truly went out to Kara. Misty had first-hand knowledge of the pain the girl was in—it hurt, perhaps more acutely than any physical ailment, to have people believe one's truest desires to be ridiculous. Her partner in conversation's attitude only increased her need to make life better for Kara however she might be able to. To begin accomplishing this goal, she kept her anger in check as she responded. "Yes, kids will be kids. Much more than Kara's wish troubles me. She confided that the opportunity for adoption has been limited by her disability and she's tired of seeing the joy this brings to her friends while she doesn't ever get to share in it. There has to be something you can do," the princess pleaded.

Betsy shook her head. "I'm afraid she's right," she explained, regret spreading into her voice. "She was placed here following her birth and, over the years, I've tried to place her numerous times, but it's proven impossible to find a family both willing to care for a young person with her needs, and capable of doing so, in whichever way that applies. It's one thing to want to help; it's another entirely to be able to lift her, bathe her, take her to appointments, all of that." The older woman held Misty's gaze. "You, of all people, should understand that."

The princess forced her features to emit only graciousness as she rebuked icily, "Actually, with all due respect, you're mistaken about almost every point you made. Not to mention, I refuse to accept that no family in Mooncrest, or a neighboring kingdom for that matter, can bring Kara up with relative ease."

Betsy avoided eye contact with Misty for a second, before bristling indignantly, "What are you saying?"

Misty held out her upturned palms, a gesture designed to placate, returning to her claim. "I want to help Kara. She wasn't lying when she said that I'm close with Prince Derrick. He obviously has considerable pull within this realm and, if you'll let me combine your resources with his, I'm sure I can find her a suitable family."

The princess's audience of one crossed her legs over one another, tapping her foot against the floor in a show of impatience at Misty's pause.

"I'm currently staying with the prince," Misty elaborated after some time, putting on a brave face and ignoring her racing heartbeat. "Allow

Kara to stay with us for a while. I'll make some inquiries, detailing her circumstances as thoroughly as I can in light of the similarities we share. Should I encounter promising candidates, Kara and I will move forward with interviews together."

Betsy moved her head at the same pace as Misty's words, as if the constant motion rendered information clearer for her. In light of the director's taciturn, pessimistic attitude, Misty suspected the woman would never permit the plan she'd just outlined to take effect. She momentarily froze when she received a thumbs-up as a critique. "It's unorthodox but, strangely, wonderful."

The princess flashed her first unforced grin since they'd started talking. "Thank you."

"Well, normally, I wouldn't condone anything of this sort, but I'm certain that she'll be safe in the castle." The curly-haired woman didn't end her thoughts there. "Plus, once she concedes that not even royal connections can get her what she wants, she'll have to live in the real world with the rest of us."

Misty balked at the revelation that her proposal was being viewed as a doomed experiment, working to clamp down on her sparking temper. She sucked in a lungful of air, mentally counted to ten, and grit out, "Well, I should be going."

"I expect so, and Kara's free to go as well. Please keep your intentions to yourself until you've departed. I don't want to cause a stir among the children. I'll send you contact information for a few potential placements, as well as her clothes, as soon as I can," Betsy proffered.

"That'd be much appreciated. Thank you for your time," Misty stated cordially, walking out of Betsy's office without acknowledging the woman further. She and Kara, who'd been keeping vigil outside the door, came within a split second of running into each other like bumper cars before she veered to the left, smiling dazzlingly. "I'm about to head home—and you're coming with me!" she all but gushed.

Kara blinked, amazed. "Wait, what? What about Betsy? She was really mad at me. I am in for it this time. I'm sure of it."

Misty laughed at the lilt of genuine disappointment in the girl's voice. "Don't be silly. You have her permission to come with me. Let's go." Misty wasn't convinced that things would go smoothly once they began their trip, but there was no retreating now. "It'll be fun!"

Kara waved her off with a grin. "You don't have to sell me on it. I'll go just about anywhere to leave this place in the dust."

With that, the two of them exited Mooncrest Group Home, heading in the direction of the castle. As they walked, Misty debated the best tactic to use when imparting the highlights of the past couple of hours to Derrick. Springing another unexpected house-guest on him wasn't exactly an appropriate reimbursement for the hospitality he'd shown her. Given that Kara was next to her at this very moment, though, she would have to do it as gently as possible and leave it at that. In keeping with this mindset, when she and her visitor reached their destination, Dex and Cliff were entrusted with entertaining Kara while Misty prepared the prince for what lay in store.

Chapter Nine

Misty was astounded upon finding Derrick not in bed, but in the studio, dancing.

"That was quite the miraculous recovery," she kidded, watching him move through the routine that was becoming more ingrained in her with each viewing.

Derrick's body jolted at the unanticipated interruption and he hurriedly shut off his accompaniment. "Hey, sweetie. I didn't expect you back this soon. How'd it go?"

Misty frowned. "We'll get to that. Right now, I'm interested in you. Spill."

The prince took her hand. "I was never sick."

"You think?" Misty retorted. "What I don't understand is why you felt you had to lie to me."

"I wanted you to handle my audiences so you could see that you're capable of running a kingdom." He paused, giving her time to mull over the news he'd just disclosed before soldiering on. "I figured you'd never agree without there being a little alarm involved, so my staff and I got a little creative around here this morning." He shrugged apprehensively, his admission blurring the line between statement and question.

Which explains their strange behavior. All the pieces clicked for Misty as she silently came to this conclusion; she chided herself for not reaching it sooner. "This—all of it—is my parents' fault. If they'd made me worldly, I wouldn't have fallen for your tricks," she mumbled.

Derrick laughed, his brows furrowing. "Did you say something?"

Misty shook her head fast enough to have her hair fly in her face. "Nope. What you did does make sense and it did force me to broadened, so to speak. Honesty is the best policy, though."

"I know, sweetie. I won't lie to you again. I promise. So? Tell me how today went," he insisted, hope in his eyes.

"It didn't go as well as you probably would've liked," she revealed quietly.

The prince brought his hand up to frame her face. "That's okay. It was only your first try. Do them for a month straight, and you'll be a pro."

Misty nodded appreciatively and grinned. "I told your chocolatier and your florist to open a joint shop and make the business a success together." Misty inhaled, steeling for what she had to say next. "I brought a little girl home, too," she rushed casually.

"It sounds like you did gre—" Derrick arrested partway through the commendation, the last group of words taking that long to register. "Say that again, please."

Misty clearly summarized Kara's plight, heavily underscoring her own role in it.

"Sweetheart, I know you feel responsible, but you don't have to take in an orphan. That's a *huge* commitment," Derrick warned.

"I'm aware. I'm not talking permanently. I'm helping her find a family. That's it. I kept picturing her sitting in that place while I did," she lowered her eyes, puffed out a breath, and locked a more resolute gaze with his. "If you want to make up for lying to me, you can welcome her here for a few days. Otherwise, Dex and I are going to take Kara somewhere else. No one deserves to be alone, Derrick." Her shoulders slumped under the weight of her declaration but, nonetheless, she held her position.

Derrick gripped her shoulders tightly, drawing her attention to him and sustaining it, ensuring he would be heard. "No one is going anywhere, Misty. I love you and I want you here. Both you and Dex. If Kara being here is that important to you, she can stay as long as she needs to."

Misty's demeanor brightened almost instantly. "You mean that?"

Derrick touched her cheek. "Of course. Also, in the interest of being truthful, while you look lovely and like true nobility today, your natural look is just as alluring. You don't need any of that stuff that you have on right now. You're gorgeous without it."

The princess nodded. "I'll try to remember that for the future."

"I'm only reiterating the facts," he imparted sagely, leaning down and pressing his lips to hers.

When they broke apart and their pulses slowed to a normal rhythm, it was time for Derrick to meet Kara.

* * *

Misty cleared her throat to get Kara's attention as she and Derrick approached her.

Turning her head at the sound, the little girl smiled at the pair before launching a tennis ball across the lawn. "Hi."

The princess returned the grin easily, Cliff and Dex raucously pursuing their target providing an interesting soundtrack to the moment. Kara giggled, as she followed their progress, the movement exposing her dimples. "I see the three of you are becoming fast friends," Misty observed.

The little girl nodded as Dex brought the ball back to her.

Misty stopped Kara from throwing the ball a second time with a soft hand on her shoulder. "Sweetheart, how about you take a break? I want to introduce you to my friend Derrick."

The little girl laughed. "I live in a group home, not under a rock. The older girls have major crushes on your *friend*." Kara rolled her eyes. "Trust me. I know who he is."

Derrick stepped around Misty. "If there's one thing I hate, it's being out of the loop. I can't wait to get to know you as well as you seem to know me. Besides, any friend of Misty's is a friend of mine," he smiled affectionately. "You can stay here in the castle with us for as long as you like."

Biting her lip, Kara eyed him warily. "Are you sure? It's hard work having me around."

The prince wrote off her fears with a flourish of his hand. "The most strenuous activity in my life at the moment is keeping these two," he tilted his head toward Cliff and Dex, "occupied." He shook his head in mock disapproval of the duo. "Having you around will be the perfect change of pace," he pledged.

Kara's posture relaxed. "Okay. I can keep tabs on them for you."

Misty beamed as she took all of this in, light and happiness filling her heart. *Things are already improving for Kara. I just hope they stay that way*, she mused. "Then it's settled! You'll live here until we find the best family in the kingdom for you."

The little girl stroked Dex's head enthusiastically as he settled next to her, Cliff perched on his back as per usual. "What about my stuff? Are we going back to get it?"

Misty negated these questions with a shake of her head. "Don't worry, sweetie. Betsy said she'd send it as soon as she could."

"Awesome," Kara replied. "Today must be my lucky day. I get to stay in a castle and avoid a punishment." she smiled brightly.

The princess shook her head again, denial in the gesture. "Not so fast. You still deserve to face the consequences of your actions. After supper, you'll sit and write Betsy an apology letter," she instructed, channeling her mother as she had earlier in the day. It was necessary to reprimand Kara, but Misty felt like a hypocrite when the words came out; she'd just commanded a little girl to write a missive similar to the one she'd yet to compose to her parents. Despite the difficulty of doing so, Misty pushed this aside and kept her resolve intact.

Kara glanced at the prince, seeking confirmation. "I wasn't there for whatever event you ladies are discussing, but I agree with Misty," he asserted.

Kara puffed out a submissive breath. "I'll get on it after we eat. What're we having?"

The princess put a pensive finger to her chin. "Chicken fingers, french fries, and brownies…sound good?"

"Yep. Three of my favorite foods at one time!" the little girl twirled her wheelchair in an ecstatic loop, bringing up the rear of the group as everyone made their way inside to await dinner.

***

Five days later, Misty came home from her follow-up with the quarreling Mooncrest businessmen to find Derrick setting all the fixings for a spaghetti dinner on the table while Kara did her homework at the counter behind him.

As soon as Derrick noticed her arrival, his face lit up. "Hey. How was your day, sweetie?"

"Great! Thomas and Maurice have had excellent sales so far and, if the trend continues, they're on track to be booming in a couple of months. I'm so glad everything's working out for them," Misty sighed contentedly, sliding up to her usual spot at the table.

Derrick's smiled widened. "I wasn't expecting anything less. Your idea was brilliant."

"I don't know if I would go as far as to say brilliant, but I won't stop you," she laughed. "Seriously, though. It means a lot that you think so."

"You probably shouldn't be so lovey-dovey around the food," Kara joked, clearing her workspace.

Derrick shoved the little girl's shoulder playfully as Misty simultaneously ruffled her hair.

"How was school today?" Derrick asked her as he loaded plates with spaghetti, salad, and garlic bread.

After taking a bite of pasta, the little girl answered, "Good. We got our math tests back."

The princess sat up a bit straighter at that. "What's the verdict, sweetheart?" she asked.

"I got an A," the young girl divulged in an undertone.

Misty and Derrick leaned toward Kara, scrutinizing her.

"What was that, sweetie?" the princess prompted urgently.

The prince laughed. "If you leave us hanging much longer, I don't think she'll," he hooked a thumb in his girlfriend's direction, "make it."

"I got a 98%," Kara announced proudly, beaming.

"That's definitely one for the win column. High-five." Derrick held up a hand in invitation and his guest bridged the inches that separated them, completing the act.

"Awesome! I'm so proud of you!" the princess exclaimed.

Crunching on a crouton from her salad, Misty brought Derrick's attention away from Kara when she asked, "Anything noteworthy happen to you today? We have to start keeping up with this one, here," she pointed her fork at their young cohort.

As the three of them continued eating and chatting easily about their lives, Misty considered the speed with which they'd fallen into seamless domestic bliss. Their current pleasure in each other's company made her somewhat hesitant to begin her search for a family for Kara. However, she knew the little girl needed permanent stability, not just a temporary fix. After supper, she put feelers out to the prospective adoptive families whose information she'd finally gotten from Betsy a few days before. An hour of conversing with these people left her with very mixed emotions about the three interviews she'd set up. Pinching the bridge of her nose and collecting herself as much as she could, she made her way to Kara's room to update her.

"Come in," the little girl called in response to Misty's knock.

When the door opened and revealed that Kara was once again playing fetch with Dex, Misty's heart constricted. She reached out to pet the dog, in part, to conceal her sentimentality. "You're really getting spoiled lately, aren't you, huh?"

"He deserves to be spoiled," Kara declared. Then, she switched gears rapidly. "What's up?"

"You and I are going to be spending Saturday at the zoo getting to know several families who may want to give you a home."

In that second, Derrick materialized at Misty's side to lend moral support. He gathered her hand in his, waggling his eyebrows at Kara to get a laugh out of her. "Correction: Misty and I'll both be there with you. My schedule can be rearranged just like that." He punctuated the last two words by snapping his fingers.

Derrick had been nothing but kind to Misty since she'd come into his life. He'd been there for her and Kara whenever they needed him, and yet, her letter to her parents had remained unwritten. Over the past few weeks, the princess had made a couple of efforts to sit down and put words to paper but, each time, she'd hated the final product and tossed it in the wastebasket. She'd centered her focus on helping Kara, and others in Mooncrest who required it, instead of that infernal letter. The passage of time hadn't diminished Misty's guilt in the slightest, even with her tireless work. Not wanting to give her insecurities away to Kara and Derrick, the princess glued a smile on her face throughout their tiny unit's viewing of *Cinderella* in the castle theater later that evening.

Chapter Ten

Saturday came more quickly than any of them wanted it to. Misty smiled as the three of them emerged from the castle and she saw that the prince had arranged for the same horse-drawn carriage he'd procured for their first date to carry them today. Her smile caved in seconds later as both her and Kara's wheelchairs careened into her memory.

One look at Kara let her know that the child shared her thoughts, and Misty was crushed by the fact that she'd, however inadvertently, caused her pain.

"Why the long faces, darlings? You both need to trust me a little more. I've got this," he assured them confidently.

With that, the prince bent down, scooped Kara up into his arms, and sat her on the carriage's bench-seat. A moment later, he repeated this with Misty, brushing a kiss against her lips before placing her across from Kara and sliding next to her.

Misty grinned warmly as Derrick slung his arm across her shoulders. "This is great, Derrick, it really is. What about our wheelchairs, though? They're a necessary evil."

He scoffed good-naturedly. "Didn't you hear what I just said?" Seconds later, an additional, much larger, vehicle parked behind theirs, a burly man with salt and pepper hair stepping out and loading their wheelchairs, barely having to exert himself to do so. Derrick tracked the proceeding with satisfaction.

Misty, Kara, and Derrick met the first potential family for Kara at the zoo's ticket booth, surprised to see the clan clocked in at nine, seven children and two adults. Worse yet, they were all wearing identical neon green-and-white plaid outfits that had them sticking out like sore thumbs. The mother, a plump woman in her mid-40s with frizzy red hair and far too much pink lipstick on her teeth, immediately kneeled in front of Kara and began rubbing sunscreen into her skin. "You poor little thing. I just wanna hug the stuffing out of you!" the woman made good on her overzealous welcome then, yanking a squirming Kara towards her and squeezing tightly, smearing white gel on the back of the girl's dress.

The unwilling victim of this attack coughed weakly. "You're choking me," she croaked, trying in vain to extract her limbs from the grasp in which they continued to be clutched.

The woman released her with a start, gawking in utter disbelief at what was taking place before her. "You can talk!"

Kara widened her eyes pointedly at Misty and Derrick. "Help," she mutely begged.

Misty flung herself forward, effectively cutting off the candidate's access to Kara. "It's Shirley, right?" she inquired needlessly. "I'm Misty. We spoke on the phone the other day."

Shirley seemed bewildered by this, as evidenced by her eyes and mouth popping out. "Goodness me, and here I was, assuming you were just another crippled orphan."

Misty started to form a reply but, honestly, had no way of rationally responding to what she'd witnessed. Derrick, on the other hand, had no such difficulties.

"Ma'am, you are on dangerous ground!" he shouted, loud enough to send Misty's body into a spasm. "There is no excuse for such derogatory language, in this company or any other," he added in a lower, more authoritative tone, rubbing Misty's back, endeavoring to calm her rigid muscles.

The father, a balding, heavyset man whose breath smelled of pipe tobacco, finally chimed in. "Uh, I'm Ralph, Shirley here's husband. Your Majesty, please pardon my wife. She didn't mean any offense to anyone." Ralph nodded toward his children. "As you can see, we've got a lot of youngsters." He flashed a brief, nervous half-smile. "Every one of 'em's adopted and, well, we've been asked to take in cri—, " biting his lip to stop himself short, Ralph went with a different choice of words, "—people like Kara before, and none of them have been able to speak, so to get acquainted with two who can? Shirl was taken aback, is all," he explained with another grin.

The prince nodded as he took this in. "Taken aback or not, her words will not be tolerated another time." He paused momentarily, considering the best way to proceed. He glanced at Kara and Misty before returning to Ralph. "If you and your wife cannot see any of these ladies' stunning qualities other than their ability to converse with you, your family isn't the right fit for Kara. We have an engagement. Enjoy your day at the zoo," the prince concluded emphatically yet diplomatically. Offering the familial group a curt up and down motion of his head in parting, he turned and left them in the dust. Misty and Kara smirked, said goodbye in unison, and rushed to catch up with him.

"Okay, Derrick. Give it up," Kara demanded once they were out of earshot of any possible audiences.

He peered at her incredulously. "I don't understand."

"Where've you been hiding your white horse? You went into full-on 'prince charming' mode with that speech."

"I did, did I?" he laughed.

"Honestly, I'm shocked," she teased, giggling.

"That hurts, Kara." Derrick put a hand to his chest and threw his head back dramatically, pretending that he'd taken a knife to the gut. "If you'll recall, my horse is brown and, last I checked, I am already a prince. The charming part is a bit up in the air, though," he shot back.

Misty, who'd been keeping tabs on Derrick and Kara's exchange thus far, moved toward him, folded their hands together, and jumped to add. "I, for one, find you quite charming, and I hope you'll always be my prince."

Putting heartening weight into their combined grip, Derrick kissed her cheek. "You bet."

Kara focused on the concrete beneath her, making a show of faux-gagging. "Yep. Prince Charming's definitely here to stay."

* * *

By the time they'd taken care of Kara's fervent request to feed the monkeys and koalas, the second interview of the day was mere minutes away.

These candidates were supposedly a young thirty-something couple accompanied by the husband's parents. However, to Misty's mystification, the duo that approached them fit neither of these descriptions. Judging by the appearance of the people in front of her, if they had children of their own then they could no longer be classified as such; they were, undoubtedly, fully-grown adults who were well into their fifties. The woman was shorter than the princess, standing a meager 4'9". She wore glasses wide enough that they obscured her whole face from view and had a distinctively aged blue tint to her white locks. The man was tall, skinny, wore wire frames that made his eyes beady, and had more hair on his arms than on his head. He was frail, but held a hand to the small of his wife's back to give her protection. He addressed Derrick first. "Hello, I'm Fred. This is my wife, Edna. So nice to meet you, your majesty."

Derrick smiled, grasping Fred's hand. "There's no need to be that formal. Call me Derrick, and it's nice to meet you as well. This is my girlfriend, Misty," Derrick proudly established.

Misty's features brightened at this, her heartbeat doing cartwheels at Derrick's choice of moniker. *I don't know if I'll ever get use to him calling me that,* she marveled silently, repeating Derrick's gesture with Edna's husband from a moment ago with the lady herself. "It's great that you could make it out this afternoon. I'm Misty—the woman who initially spoke with you."

Edna nodded politely. "Of course, dear. I remember."

Misty turned her gaze on the little girl standing behind her. "This is Kara, the reason we're all here."

The elderly pair followed suit, glancing toward Kara, grinning widely. "Nice to meet you, little lady," Fred offered graciously.

"Likewise, sir," the second-grader replied.

Shaking his head to refute some part of what she'd said, he chuckled. "I'm no sir, honey. Call me Fred."

Edna signaled her agreement, beaming so brightly that the expression reached her eyes. "Clown would be more accurate," she joked. "You're free to call me Edna."

Kara fought to keep from laughing at how the woman labeled her spouse. "Well, I'm pleased to meet both of you."

"If I'm prodding you too much, forgive me, but—I was under the impression that your son and daughter-in law would be joining us. Are they coming?" the princess spoke as kindly as was possible when delving for un-volunteered facts.

Edna opened her mouth to speak, but nothing emerged. Fred stepped in, focusing downward in order to get a better lock on his intended message. "No, no one'll be joining us," he revealed in a whisper, his expression inundated with sorrow.

"Well, that's all right. We'll meet them soon. Let's have lunch at the café, shall we?"

"Yes, let's," Derrick concurred, heading up the small group's path in that direction.

Everyone chatted familiarly over pepperoni pizza in the zoo café for several minutes before Fred and Edna pulled Derrick and Misty aside.

"I thought it was time we address the elephant in the room," Fred started once they were away from Kara. "We're older than you expected."

From her spot next to her husband, Edna moved her head up and down vigorously. "I'm sorry we led you to believe that our son and daughter-in-law were going to be available to meet you. Truth be told, we don't have children. Not anymore." This was delivered calmly, but the aloofness didn't extend to her features and body language; these were filled with anguish.

Fred drew Edna into his side and hugged her softly. "We had a child, about 30 years ago. Lexi was our miracle baby. Remarkable in every way." He broke off, moisture clouding his eyes. "She had needs similar to Kara's. She had a tough life filled with pain and surgery, but you'd never have known that. She was the happiest little thing on the planet and she brought tremendous joy to us. We'd have the exact same experience again, in a heartbeat, even though we lost her." He coughed, dislodging the lump that had formed in his throat, before he went on. "We know that that's not possible, but we thought helping Kara might help us," Fred choked out, a single tear rolling down his cheek. Misty sobbed at that but, before she could get any words out, Edna cut in. "Spending the day with all of you has made us see that thinking we could do this was silly—Kara deserves to have young, vibrant parents. We've so enjoyed meeting you, though, and we truly hope you're not angry with us for stretching the truth like we did."

Misty rushed forward to embrace Edna. "Of course we're not angry," she promised. Fred nodded his gratitude and offered a momentary upturn of the corners of his mouth. "Good. We couldn't bear to upset such wonderful people."

Derrick shook his head rapidly back and forth, his features contorting as he struggled to restrain his emotions. "We've loved meeting you, as has Kara. You're both invited to visit us at the castle anytime. In fact, we insist." He hesitantly reached for Fred, pulling him in for a one-armed hug and patting his shoulder kindly.

As Misty released Edna from her hold, she breathed, "Yes! Kara would love to see you and we'll make sure this can still happen with the new family."

"Sounds great. We wouldn't miss any chance to do that for the world," Edna and Fred assured their newfound friends.

With that, the four adults put smiles on their faces and went back to Kara. The elderly couple bid a quick 'see you later', pledging that they would visit soon. Misty and Derrick settled in to wait with Kara, preparing to meet the final family.

* * *

When the last mother had suggested meeting for ice cream at the zoo café later in the afternoon, Misty hadn't thought much of it, but as soon as the young couple arrived, star-struck beyond belief, she found herself ill at ease.

The man, boyish, his face riddled with acne, shoved his hand into Derrick's the moment they walked up, pumping the limb vigorously. "Holy crap! I can't believe it's really you! Little ol' me meeting royalty, who'd've thunk it?"

The girl standing next to him hit his arm, putting a stop to his eager physicality. "Would you chill out? You're being weird!" she hissed vehemently. Whispering something incomprehensible back, he stood up from his seat and cleared his throat. "My apologies, your majesty. This is so surreal, though, you know? I'm Jason and this," he indicated his assessor, "is Jayla, my lady friend."

Derrick smiled at the girl to whom he'd just been introduced. "It's nice to meet you both. There's no need for formalities—call me Derrick." Contentment spread further across his face when he looked back at the girls standing beside him. "This is Misty," he informed, brushing his hand against her shoulder. "And this is the famous Kara." He put an affectionate arm around his charge.

Jayla's brows came together to form a single entity. "Who?"

"Kara? The little girl who needs a family? We talked about this," Misty reminded her, a forced polite smile plastered across her face.

It took some time for comprehension to dawn on Jayla. "Oh, riiiiight," she breathed, elongating the last syllable.

Jason chuckled haughtily. "We remember. She's just playin.'" Going down to Kara's level, he volunteered, "Hey, cutie. How about some ice cream? You'd like that, right?" his tone was tailored to a baby, a fact that left Kara and Misty cringing.

"Yep, that I do, big guy!" the little girl volleyed in a spot-on imitation of Jason. It had no effect on him whatsoever.

"What's the best part of being royalty?" Jayla queried Derrick as they all sat down with their frozen treats.

His answer was instantaneous. "I love how much of a difference I can make in the lives of my subjects."

Their unofficial interviewer focused on Misty next. "What about you, princess?"

Misty stared at her in shock. "Excuse me?"

Jason elbowed Jayla in the side. "Ow. I,—I mean what have you enjoyed most during your time here?" she amended rapidly.

The princess's eyes narrowed as she deduced that something was indeed going on with these people.

96 • Just the Way You Are

"How exactly did you know I'd been visiting? I never mentioned that to you."

Jayla averted her eyes, a picture of guilt. "Just a lucky guess—I guess."

Derrick interrupted then, saving Misty the trouble of replying to Jayla's inane deflection. He stared the newcomers down, no leniency visible. "Why don't we stop playing this game; tell us what's really happening here. Without any lies." His pitch granted no room for argument.

Jayla hung her head, Jason releasing a loud gush of air behind her before addressing Kara using the babyish tone he'd gone with earlier. "Promise you won't be sad when you hear what we're about to say, okay?"

Kara rolled her eyes heavenward. "Quit worrying and do as you're told, okay, dummy?" Jason's face wrinkled in indignation as he closed his mouth quickly. Jayla watched this, let out a huff of frustration, turned to Misty, and spoke. "Don't be mad, your majesties. You see, princess, we're from Starryton. We're only doing what your father demanded of us," she revealed.

Misty's head spun, her mouth going desert-dry. "Wha—what d'you mean what my father wants?"

Sensing her distress at the same moment, Derrick took her hand, while Kara shot a supportive smile her way. She also tilted her head at the partially-melted ice cream in front of the princess, reminding her friend that it was there. After eating a tiny spoonful to center herself, Misty made another attempt to get some clues. "What's going on?"

Fixing her gaze on everything she could find other than her interrogator, Jayla answered, "Misty, when you ran away, your father figured that you'd come here, but no one knew how to locate you. As you know, the royal guard from our kingdom is banned here," she elaborated meekly. "When you hadn't returned after a few days, King Reginald implored that citizens who had contacts in Mooncrest get in touch with him or Queen Eliza regarding your safety and whereabouts."

Holding up a hand, Derrick stopped Jayla there, gaping at Misty.

"Sweetie, what is she talking about? I thought you wrote your parents a letter."

Misty stared at the ground. "I'm so sorry. I tried to write it, really I did. Nothing sounded right, though. Since I couldn't seem to come up with the right words, I threw myself into helping the people of Mooncrest. I'm so sorry," she repeated earnestly, a single tear rolling down her cheek.

The prince leaned towards her, wiping at the moisture on her skin. "It's okay. I understand, and your help's been invaluable. It'll be okay, I promise. We'll figure everything out."

Misty made her best attempt at a grin. "Thank you." Regaining her composure, she nodded, returning to the matter at hand. "Go on," she commanded Jason and Jayla.

"Yes. Please continue," Derrick joined in, the glower he directed at the young couple not having lost any strength.

Clearing his throat, Jason dove first. "The florist who came to seek advice last week? The one feuding with the chocolate guy? He's my uncle." Jason let out a nervous laugh and wiped sweaty hands on his pants.

Kara rolled her eyes, sighing a dramatic huff. "Just spit it out, will ya? We haven't got all day."

Shocked by the bluntness of the youngster in front of him, he struggled to comply. "I m-mentioned that we were l-look—" He stopped as Misty leaned forward and looked him straight in the eye. "Breathe." She inhaled a deep lungful of air, demonstrating; she continued talking once he seemed to have mastered this. "No one is in trouble," she promised. "Just relax and finish your story."

A few more cleansing breaths gave Jason the resolve he needed to soldier on. "My uncle confirmed that you were here and said he had heard you were trying to find a little girl a family—which is very nice of you, by the way," he smiled, the expression fading when no one else shared the sentiment. "So we got on the phone, called the Mooncrest Group Home, pretended we were interested in adoption, and here we are," he rambled, relieved to have finished his explanation. Color drained from his face with the realization that Misty wasn't letting him off the hook.

"You're not interested in giving Kara a better life, you're just here to check up on me. Now that that's done, the next step is—? What? To return home and tell my father I'm happy and safe?"

Jason raked his hands through his hair. "Actually, princess, there's a bit more to it than that. When I confirmed that you were here, King Reginald ordered me to collect you and bring you home, even if you were kicking and screaming for the entire trip."

Before Misty could form a rebuttal, Derrick bit out a single laugh. "She's not going anywhere. You're in my kingdom; I'm the letter of the law here. Go home and tell your king that his daughter is happy and safe, as you heard the lady herself say. You can also tell him to expect an invit—"

Misty shook her head rapidly, her eyes huge and full of worry. She put a hand on Derrick's shoulder. "Sweetie, what're you doing?"

Derrick clasped her hands securely in his. "I'm simply taking matters into my own hands. I'm going to fix this. Watch my plan unfold," he whispered with pride and excitement.

She tried, however futilely to reason with him. "You don't understand. My father won't co—"

"Shhh," he mollified calmly, tightening his fingers around hers. "You trust me, don't you?"

She nodded vigorously. "Of course. But—"

"No buts, sweetheart. If you trust me, let me handle this for you. For us," he implored, the words a sweet, calm whisper.

Misty focused on Derrick, recognized hope in his eyes, and relented.

"Okay," she breathed, her shoulders deflating. Pulling her into a gentle hug, Derrick kissed her forehead before remembering Jason and Jayla. "Go back to Starryton. Tell the king that his daughter is happy and that he'll receive an invitation to my castle to see her soon. Understood?"

The pair nodded simultaneously. "Yes, your majesty!" Jason's response was quick and his head experienced no break in its movement.

With that, Jason and Jayla departed for Starryton, leaving Derrick, Misty, and Kara free to return to Mooncrest's castle.

Chapter Eleven

Restless that night, Misty used the call button Derrick had recently had installed to ask Marie for a glass of warm milk. Knowing she needed someone to talk to or, rather, to listen to her get everything off her chest, she went to enjoy her drink in the den with Dex.

"Hey, bud! I know you've been enjoying yourself here. I am too, but our time in Mooncrest may have to come to an end soon," she warned as she petted him, her eyes full of emotion.

Dex whimpered, sensing Misty's distress. She took a sip of the warm liquid she held before addressing her furry friend again.

"Oh, Dex. I'm sorry. I've been so stupid. I don't know how I got so attached so fast—first to Derrick, now to Kara." Stroking his ears, she whispered, "You should have been there today. Two of the adoptive families were complete jokes. And the other—they were great, but not right either. This whole situation has blown up in my face. I don't know what I'm going to do." She took another sip of milk, hoping it would engender calm in her.

"Sweetheart, today wasn't your fault. You have to know that. Plus, you're certainly not stupid." Derrick's voice drifted closer to her as he entered the room.

She screamed at the unexpected noise, put her hand to her chest to quell her spasms, and faced him.

"I'm so sorry, sweetie. I didn't mean to startle you, but something told me I'd find you with Dex." He patted the dog's head tenderly.

"I couldn't sleep and didn't want to wake you."

He brushed a finger across her cheek. "Sweetie, you can always talk to me, whatever time it is. Plus, I've been wanting to talk to you myself."

"What, pray tell, is on your mind?"

Sighing in relief, he took her hand in his. "I need to tell you something." His voice betraying none of the nerves Misty knew lingered below the surface; this made her that much more apprehensive about what was coming.

"What is it?"

"My parents will be home in a few days for my mother's birthday."

She nodded. "Yep, I remember. I'm really looking forward to meeting them." She forced a grin, avoiding thinking about the prospect of meeting them for too long.

He shot her a small, contained smile in return. "Good. I'm looking forward to getting to know yours too. I put their invitation to the celebratory dinner in the mail today."

Misty gasped, shocked. "You what? Derrick! You know the history between our families! Why would you do that without asking me?" she shouted, the words coming out much louder than she intended them to.

"Shhh," he calmed, putting a finger to his lips. "You're gonna wake Kara."

"Crap." The princess sighed, her voice back to being quiet, but taking on a frustrated edge. "It's just, I really want your parents to like me. They won't if my parents are here. They'll fight with your parents the whole time, stopping just in time to take me home." Misty pushed forward in spite of the color rising in her face. "My parents aren't accepting like your parents or Fred and Edna. They have certain expectations, and—" Misty stopped at the feel of Derrick's hands on her shoulders.

"Sweetie, take a breath. You trust me, right? So trust me when I say that it is best we get everything out in the open." He wrapped her in a strong hug. "It'll all be fine. No one's going to take you away from me, and my parents are going to love you—because I love you."

"I love you, too," Misty sighed contentedly. "I'm going to buzz Marie. We need a little shut-eye before we start making even bigger decisions and not remembering them."

"No need to bother Marie," Derrick told her, scooping her up, kissing her forehead, and carrying her off to bed.

* * *

The next morning, Misty wasn't surprised that Derrick was already in the dance studio; she was, however, intrigued by the fact that he and Kara were dancing to Rodgers and Hammerstein's "In My Own Little Corner". She intruded, exuding delight, at the start of the second verse. "What are you two up to?"

What does it look like?" Kara giggled. She beamed, the prince holding one of her hands as she circled her wheelchair with the other.

Derrick threw his head back and laughed as he watched her go into a wheelie. "C'mon, join us!"

The princess waved him away. "Nah. That's okay," she declined. "I'd rather watch."

The prince grinned impishly, grabbed her joystick, and propelled her forward. "I'm not taking 'no' for an answer. Dance with me, beautiful."

Hanging her head, she mumbled, "No, really. I can't."

Derrick sighed, putting a hand on Kara's shoulder. "Sweetheart, you keep practicing. We'll be right back, okay?"

Kara nodded, positioning herself so that she could watch her progress in the wall-length mirror.

In the next breath, Derrick led Misty back to their spot from the previous night. "Sweetheart, Kara and I were having so much fun back there. Why wouldn't you join us? I thought you liked to dance."

Misty averted her gaze from his. "You're right. I loved dancing with you, but I'm not sure I can like *this*," she admitted.

"What do mean, sweetie?"

The princess swept a hand down her body in illustration, fighting to keep tears at bay. "In this wheelchair."

"That makes no sense. You know that, right?" Derrick admonished. "Did you not see Kara and I dancing together a few minutes ago?"

Misty focused on her lap with an unblinking intensity, tears finally escaping from her eyes. "That's different. She's a child. She doesn't—"

"That's right, sweetie." Derrick wiped the moisture from her cheeks, his tone soothing despite his interruption. "She *is* a child. A young, impressionable child." With a finger under her chin, he locked eyes with her in a firmer manner. "She had a very tough day yesterday. All of us did. I thought dancing might be a good outlet for her—I was right. You saw her in there. She was ecstatic!" the prince's mood was buoyed for a second by this mental image, but he became serious in a heartbeat. "Until you wouldn't dance, that is."

Misty's eyes released a monsoon of fresh tears. "I don't want to discourage her. I know I'm not a dancer, though. I didn't want to pretend I was." The confession rolled off her tongue as smoothly as gravel.

Derrick put an arm around her shoulder, comforting and sure. "What makes you think you're not a beautiful dancer?"

She looked up at him forlornly. "I enjoy dance, but my mother always said that I shouldn't. She assumed my tires would get in the way of the other performers on the floor."

Derrick pulled her tightly into his side. "Misty, with all due respect to your mother, that's ridiculous."

"I know," she agreed. "It all goes back to my parents keeping me in a tower and hiding my disability for years on end. They never wanted to take the chance that the family would appear weak to the citizens of Starryton."

"I'm sure your parents had good intentions in doing what they did. They've given you a warped idea of life with a disability, though." The prince gently broke away to say, "I haven't told you this yet, but I think now is the right time. My great-grandfather had polio. When my sister and I were kids, he always instilled in us that people with disabilities can do whatever able-bodied people can. They just have to do it a little differently."

Wiping her eyes on her sleeve, Misty attempted a watery grin.

Derrick smiled back at her. "It's important that you believe that message yourself and work to show younger people with disabilities that they are capable of achieving amazing things."

"How'd you get to be so smart?" Misty asked, teasing and matter-of-fact all at once.

This was met with a chuckle. "Pure luck. Now, please come and dance with me?"

No longer able to resist the effect of his combined words of wisdom and bright smile, Misty reluctantly followed Derrick into the studio.

Her face broke into a thrilled smile when he turned on the fairy lullaby from *A Midsummer Night's Dream* almost as soon as they crossed the threshold.

Kara rolled her eyes, laughing. "What is it with you and this song?"

"I'll take that to mean that you've never experienced *A Midsummer Night's Dream*. I love it because, in the end and against all odds, true love prevails."

"Cheesy," the little girl faux-coughed.

Derrick hid a laugh in clearing his throat. "Less talking, more dancing."

Misty grinned, taking his hand. "Lead the way, sir."

The prince found Kara with his gaze. "Watch so you'll be ready when I take you for another spin around the dance floor, sweetheart."

"Remember. It's not about the steps, it's about feeling the music. Just relax," he leaned forward to whisper into her ear.

Despite her reservations, Misty couldn't help but let some of the prince's enthusiasm seep into her. In mere minutes, she was executing various ballet positions with her free hand and twirling at several speeds as he kept pace with her. Kara looked on in amazement, laughing happily when the prince finally pulled her onto the dance floor, giving her Misty's place.

The princess went to bed that night blissfully at ease, having spent the day laughing and enjoying Kara and Derrick's company as they all glided around the dance studio.

Chapter Twelve

The next two days passed too quickly for Misty and, before she knew it, the queen's birthday had arrived. To say that the castle was abuzz with preparation was an understatement. Misty met more of the staff in three hours than she had in her entire stay up until now. She spent the morning with Marie and Shelly, perusing possible makeup, wardrobe, and handbag options while, all around them, people cooked, cleaned, and organized. When a royal blue gown, sapphire jewelry, a golden facial palette, and a simple golden clutch had made the final cut, she focused on Kara, who Marie reported was struggling with her choice of ensemble. Misty was shocked when she knocked on Kara's door and discovered a tornado of clothing scattered about.

Misty chuckled, plucking a shirt off the lampshade. "What on earth is going on in here, sweetie?"

Kara abandoned the pile she'd been sifting through and fixed the princess with a piercing glare—she should know the answer to her own question. "I have nothing to wear to dinner. All of my clothes are old and disgusting. How am I supposed to wear any of this," she flung her arm in an arc, indicating the mass of fabric, "while I dine with royalty?"

Misty chuckled again. "Technically, Derrick and I are royalty. You've worn these things to eat with us every night."

Kara huffed her displeasure. "That's different." She glanced across at her bed, away from her clothes.

Not having many other options with regard to solace, Misty hugged the little girl.

"I'll tell you what. I brought a few dresses from home. You can pick one you like and we'll have the seamstress alter it to fit you."

The little girl shook her head against Misty's chest, still in the comfort of her embrace. "I can't ask you to give one of your beautiful dresses to me," she protested.

Combing her fingers through Kara's blond ringlets in an attempt to calm the distraught child, Misty soothed, "Don't be silly. I'd give you all of my dresses if you wanted them. Us girls've gotta stick together. C'mon, let's go raid my wardrobe."

The princess's case was effective. With Kara giggling all the while, the two of them made their way to the tulip room to investigate Misty's dress collection. Eventually, their attention landed on the gown that Derrick had let Misty borrow, and later given to her. Her measurements taken, Kara agreed to let Marie style her hair while Misty took the gown to Carol, the castle's resident seamstress.

"Ouch! Why don't you just pull out all of my hair? It'd be faster" the little girl whined, sitting in front of a mirror as Marie tried to tame the blond waves with which she was faced.

Sighing, Marie discarded her brush. "Miss, how am I supposed to make you presentable if you won't permit me to finish your hair?"

Kara blew out an annoyed breath. "I shouldn't even be going to this ridiculous dinner. There's no way a homely orphan like me can be turned into anything else, even just for a night."

Marie opened her mouth to resist, shutting it with a smile as Misty entered, taking over the task. "Wow. I clearly have awesome timing. If you keep snapping at people helping you like that, soon you're not going to have any," she advised, beginning to brush the girl's hair carefully.

Hanging her head, Kara let out a rush of air. "I know. I'm sorry." The little girl raised her gaze and found Marie, standing behind Misty. "I apologize for the way I was acting a minute ago. I'm just nervous," she explained in a small, chastised voice.

Marie beamed brightly. "Apology accepted, miss. If you'll both excuse me, I'm going to polish the china and let you two talk." Touching the princess's shoulder, Marie offered another smile as she left the room.

Misty perfectly understood where her young charge was coming from with regard to her current emotions. She, too, had an abundance of nerves concerning the dinner and the desire to look her best in order to be accepted by the heads of both royal families. As a matter of fact, she'd been so wrapped up in her own fears about she and Derrick's parents coming together, she hadn't stopped to think about how nerve-wracking the prospect of this meal must be for a young girl who had, until recently, lived in a glorified orphanage. Realizing that Kara was far more apprehensive about this evening than she was, she pushed her feelings aside and attended to the little girl. Quietly completing Kara's hair, it took her several minutes to speak. "I know just the thing you need. I'll be right back," she smiled softly.

Moments later the princess returned hoping her latest idea would help to calm the little girl. "Sweetie, I don't know if you know this or not, but I am a firm believer that no formal ensemble is complete without a handbag."

Kara hung her head, her shoulders slumping slightly. "I don't have any handbags," she admitted quietly.

"I'm giving you this in addition to your dress so now you do," Misty said, excitement coloring her voice as she presented Kara with a small treasure troll covered handbag.

The little girl's eyes widened as she looked at the handbag in awe. "That's so pretty," she lightly touched one of the colorful gemstones the trolls on the handbag were adorned with. "But I can't accept it.

The princess shook her head. "Don't be silly. I am so excited for you to have it. It popped out at me while I was shopping after holding personal audiences the other day. I had a handbag very similar to it when I was around your age. It was my favorite accessory for many years so I just couldn't resist picking it up for you." Misty carefully handed Kara the handbag before she could object again. The princess then looked at the little girl in the mirror again. "There. That handbag was definitely meant for you. You look beautiful carrying it.—not at all homely," she encouraged.

The little girl chewed her bottom lip nervously as she examined her appearance in the surface before her. "Are you sure?"

The princess held both of her shoulders, bending forward to assure, "Yes, sweetie. You've got absolutely nothing to be nervous about. Just be yourself and everyone will love you."

A quiet knock brought both ladies out of their conversation. Misty smiled as Carol appeared. "Finished already?"

Carol nodded. "As a matter of fact I am," she responded happily, presenting the restructured dress.

"Oh my goodness. It's so pretty!" Kara gushed, taking in the full effect.

Carol smiled appreciatively. "I'm glad you like it. I have some other projects to get back to. I'll leave it here for you," she informed, hanging the dress on the doorknob before exiting.

Misty studied the gown, smiled, and looked to Kara. "Why don't I call Marie back and we can try this on?"

Kara grinned wide enough to bring out her dimples. "Sounds good!"

With Marie's help, the little girl was fully dressed in minutes. The emerald gown, to which Carol had added sequins in order to make it age appropriate, brought out the sparkle in the child's beautiful eyes. The final look left Misty watery-eyed.

"I'll give you guys a minute," Marie whispered, once again leaving Misty and Kara to their own devices.

Suddenly, confusion swept across the seven-year-old's features. "Uh oh. Marie's gone and you're crying. Is it really that bad?"

Misty shook her head rapidly. "No, no! No, sweetheart. You look beautiful—absolutely beautiful," she breathed, wiping a tear off her cheek.

"I agree," Derrick corroborated, walking up behind them. Jumping at the sound of his voice, Misty relaxed as her brain registered who was speaking. "Sorry, sweetie. Didn't mean to startle you. Neither of you has anything to worry about tonight. It'll be great! Every guest is going to adore you both. I do, so how could they not?"

"You're sweet," Misty said, her eyes sparkling. "I feel the same way, you know." She smiled, looking in Kara's direction, willing her to say something. She desperately wanted the little girl to express her affection, even if it would guarantee more painful heartache down the line.

"I'm not normally mushy, but I think we need a group hug," the little girl supplied, laughing in delight as the tiny group executed a perfect example of the act.

"You beauties feeling better?" Derrick murmured as they pulled apart.

The girls nodded vigorously in reply.

"Good, because our guests have arrived." He ushered the two of them out of the room and down the hall to meet their guests.

* * *

The way Derrick's face burst into utter joy the minute he opened the door for his mother sent delight straight to Misty's heart; this was somewhat dampened by the confusion the woman projected at the sight of her and Kara.

Misty watched his mother, whose expression mirrored his, kiss both of his cheeks. "Darling, it's wonderful to see you." Appraising him for a moment, the queen licked her thumb in preparation to rub away the lipstick smudge she'd just left on his skin.

Derrick rolled his eyes. "Mother, please. We have guests." He backed away, motioning toward the girls standing beside him.

His mother put her head to her heart in a picture of surprise. "Oh my, how rude of me! I'm just so happy to see you, I can't contain myself."

Derrick chuckled. "It's all right, Mother. I'd like to introduce you to these lovely ladies." Smiling, he put a hand on Misty's shoulder. "This is my girlfriend, Misty Miles." He glanced at Misty. "Sweetheart, this is my mother—Marguerite, Queen of Mooncrest."

Misty put out her hand, accompanied with a grin. "Very pleased to meet you! Hap—"

Marguerite tentatively returned the handshake, shooting a sidelong look at Derrick while she did so. "Girlfriend? We've only been gone a few weeks." Her eyes enlarged considerably a second later as something occurred to her. "Wait, did you say Miles? As in—?"

Trapped, Misty could only keep smiling.

In an attempt to alleviate the awkwardness surrounding them, Derrick kneeled down next to Kara. "We'll discuss that later, Mother. There's someone else you need to meet." His features brightened even more as he looked between his mother and the little girl. "This is the lovely Kara Kyle, an awesome friend of mine."

The little girl giggled nervously in the face of this introduction, repeating Misty's earlier gesture with the queen. "It's nice to meet you. Happy birthday, your majesty," she offered sweetly.

The queen beamed brightly down at Kara. "Well, aren't you adorable—those cute little dimples and everything? Any friend of Derrick's is a friend of mine. Both of you please call me Marguerite." she glanced between her son and Misty. "Forgive my earlier rudeness. I was simply a bit taken aback. I *am* an old woman, after all," the queen joked.

"You aren't old, and there was nothing rude about your demeanor," Misty promised.

"You flatter me," Marguerite deflected.

Derrick exuded contentment as he observed Misty and his mother exchanging pleasantries. "Mother, will Father be joining us at some point this evening? I really want him to meet Kara and Misty before everyone else makes an appearance."

The queen fixed him with a hard gaze. "Everyone else?"

Before he could answer the question, the queen's attention was diverted as her eyes searched the room. "Your father was right behind me. I'm not sure—"

Right at this moment, a loud crash sounded; the four of them jumped, dashing outside quickly.

* * *

"Oh God, Daddy! No! Stop!" Misty screamed frantically, as she stepped outside to find her father pushing Derrick's against an outer wall.

Despite her pleas, the two kings continued to fight, eventually rolling around, entangled, on the south lawn, in front of the moat. The queens, for their part, sobbed hysterically while Misty rushed to Kara's side and Derrick attempted to separate the battling men.

Putting one hand to his father's chest and the other to that of Starryton's monarch, he stood resolutely between them. "Somebody want to tell me what's going on?"

Derrick's father set his lips in a frustrated line, sweat dripping off of his forehead. "I caught this idiot trying to get in even though he's banned from the premises."

"He's not banned. I invited him," Derrick said, unsure of exactly what was taking place.

Reginald gritted his teeth and sneered at Archibald. "That's right. He invited me."

Archibald snorted contemptuously. "He should have known better than to invite a Miles into my domain. I'm officially sending you back the way you came."

"Father, please!" Derrick shouted, glaring sternly in the ruler's direction.

"Get off my property!" Archibald commanded Reginald, deaf to his son's entreaty.

"With pleasure. I never had any desire to visit your shabby residence. I only came to collect my daughter." Here, his iron scrutiny located Misty in the crowd. "We're going."

Misty's heartbeat reverberated through her chest with enough strength to leave her worried about enclosing it, but she knew if she didn't stand up to her father now, she never would. *This can't be like the letter*, she scolded herself. *I can't give up. I have to stand up to him.* Armed with an encouraging nod from Derrick, she took a deep breath and stared her father down.

"No, Daddy. I'm staying here."

Letting out an enraged roar of a laugh, her father took hold of her arm. "You will do no such thing." He tightened his grip demonstratively. "We'll discuss this when we're alone."

Derrick jumped to Misty's defense as soon as her father had finished speaking. "Sir, you are in my kingdom now and I will not allow you to speak that way to a lady or force her to do anything that is against her will."

Reginald's face steadily reddened as his anger intensified. "No one can tell me how to handle my daughter—especially not a scrawny little—"

"Daddy, that's enough!" Misty yelled, gaining the attention of everyone around her with her tone. The princess only wanted to protect her prince as he'd done for her moments ago. She didn't comprehend the daunting nature of her task until six pairs of eyes bore into her.

She closed her own, inhaled a centering breath, and started. "I love Derrick, and he—"

"Sweetie, you don't have to—" Derrick interrupted kindly albeit hastily.

Misty put a finger against his lips, cutting him off. "Shh, Derrick, I have to do this," she insisted.

"Okay." Derrick grinned proudly, gesturing for her to continue.

Ignoring her nerves, she began again, her voice shaking. "I love Derrick, and he loves me. We asked you all here to both commemorate Queen Marguerite's birthday and to tell you we're a couple."

The minute that last word left her mouth, her parents' expressions turned horrified, but she persevered. "I'm not going anywhere with you, Daddy. This has become my home. I'm going to stay here and assist Derrick in reigning over Mooncrest when the time comes." She grinned nervously, waiting for a response.

Reginald released another roar of laughter, a vein protruding from his forehead with the sound. "That's preposterous! How can you possibly know what love is? There's also the fact that you cannot reign over any kingdom, but particularly not this one."

The princess dismissed his statement with a slight shake of her head. "No, Daddy, it's actually not at all out of the ordinary. I've come to understand that love means accepting people as they are. Meeting Derrick opened my eyes and my mind. I don't blame you or Mama—for a while I didn't even love myself. Things are different now, though. As I said, this is my home, and I can't go anywhere with you. I won't." Misty had stopped shouting, but was, instead, struggling to get words out around the tears that had begun to fall.

Misty's mother responded before the king had a chance to.

"How can you say we don't love you?" the queen wavered, her eyes brimming with wetness of their own. "You're our whole world. We've done everything for you." She shook her head in disbelief, sobbing.

"Yes, Mama, you and Daddy did everything except encourage me to live life to the fullest," the princess explained. Sucking in a breath, she wiped fresh tears from her face, pressing onward. "I've only ever wanted to reign over a kingdom half as well as you and Daddy have, but you guys had me believing that I couldn't because of my disability. I had to vanquish Trovella to realize that I can do anything I set my mind to, even with the challenges I face." Her lips lifted upward in a faint grin at the memory of defeating the enemy.

Worry and uncertainty replaced whatever emotions her parents and Derrick's had been experiencing prior to Trovella's name rolling off of her tongue.

Archibald's eyes bugged out of his head. "What are you talking about?" he hissed urgently.

"If you'll all come inside and have dinner with us, I'll be delighted to tell you." Misty face remained demure and unassuming as she winked at Derrick.

After a few more minutes of negotiation, both families reluctantly stepped inside to dine together.

* * *

Bernie and the other members of the Denison family's staff served the seven dinner attendees a beautiful meal of pot roast, asparagus, and rolls shortly after they entered the dining room. The clang of forks hitting plates was the only sound in the room for what could have been an eternity, and felt as much to the princess. "Derrick cooked dinner. Isn't it delicious?" she asked, finally breaking the oppressive silence.

Reginald chuckled sarcastically. "Mooncrest's number one chef is too lazy to cook now?"

Archibald slammed his fork on the table and stood up to defend himself. "How dare you come into my castle and call me lazy!" he bellowed. "That's the epitome of disrespect." His face took on a purple cast the more he shouted. "No wonder your daughter wants to stay here."

Reginald's turn to stand came then, the man leaning forward and bringing himself and his adversary nose to nose. "Don't ever mention my daughter again. You're the one who's disrespectful. You're also a liar."

The two kings were soon going at it full force. When Misty couldn't stand listening to another word, she inserted herself in the middle of the verbal brawl. "Daddy, please! You don't understand. King Archibald didn't sabotage your cupcake. It was—"

Reginald glanced between his child and Archibald, sweat pouring off of him. "You're right. He didn't just ruin my cupcake—he tried to poison my father and have me blamed for it."

Derrick rushed to help the woman he loved. "Father, please. Just tell him—"

"This is ridiculous!" Marguerite's shout was the first time she'd spoken since introductions were made. "Your father has nothing to tell him. We've tried to reason with these people, and—"

"These people? All of the sudden we're 'these people'?" Eliza yelled back.

Kara chose this moment to inhale deeply and shriek 'Stop!' at the top of her lungs.

The little girl's suspicion that she'd been forgotten was confirmed as the room fell silent, everyone gaping at her like she'd grown three heads.

"Did you have something you wanted to say?" Marguerite queried the little girl. Kara zeroed in on the stark white tablecloth to, clear her mind before putting herself back at center stage.

"Did you all fall asleep in History class?" the little girl surveyed the room at large in a courteous mocking voice that held no grudge against her audience; pure curiosity drove her to ask.

The royals seated around her locked bewildered stares on her. Derrick finally spoke after a long period of dead quiet. "What do you mean?"

Kara laughed. "Everyone knows that Trovella derailed the cooking competition that led Starrycrest to break into Starryton and Mooncrest 20 years ago. We talk about it in school every anniversary." She was astounded by the fact that they had no knowledge of this.

Kara sighed first at her listeners' continued confusion, then in relief when Misty voiced her agreement. "She's right. Trovella told me the whole story as a way to intimidate me the other day." Archibald glanced between Kara and Misty, his face having retained its violet color.

"Either of you want to fill in any blanks?" he asked. It came out as an order rather than a question.

Misty hesitantly relayed the tale to the families, including everything from the fulfillment of her wish to the crown jewel debacle and the eventual demise of Trovella.

For a long moment after she'd finished, both pairs of parents stared at her in shock. When her father had finally digested everything, his voice oozed skepticism. "How do you know Trovella wasn't putting you on because this clown," he jabbed a finger at Archibald, "wanted a clear conscience or something?"

The princess puffed out a disappointed breath, scowling at her father. "Think about it, Daddy. She was determined to take over our kingdoms and fill them with things out of nightmares. Do you really think she would fulfill a wish for anyone, let alone King Archibald?"

"Well, I—um—" her father stammered.

Misty didn't allow him to finish his thought. "Give it up, Daddy. They're good people. They were deceived by Trovella, just as we were. I'm not going to let you stand here in their home and insult them." The princess unknowingly addressed him with the authority that she'd gained in Mooncrest.

Silence once again descended upon the group, but Kara quickly negated it. "King Reginald, sir, I mean, your majesty—if it's evidence you're looking for, someone donated footage of the competition to Mooncrest Library about five years ago. It's probably still in there if—"

Eliza put a calming hand on Kara's shoulder. "It's okay, sweetie. We don't need any evidence aside from our daughter's words." She smiled graciously, glancing at her husband as well as Derrick's parents. "I think it's high time we let bygones be bygones. We must simply be grateful that Trovella is gone."

Derrick nodded. "I agree." He smiled, cleared his throat, and added, "I hope our families will also do more than that someday."

Before anyone could ask him to elaborate further, Bernie served dessert: tiramisu. Although they made small talk while eating it, the room was far from comfortable and, as such, heavy subjects were avoided. Despite this atmosphere, Misty's parents stayed until Queen Marguerite had opened her birthday gifts, reluctantly departing without their daughter after she promised to visit soon.

The moment the door closed behind them, Misty threw her arms around Derrick, beaming brightly. "I can't believe we just had dinner with all of them in one room and nobody lost a limb. It was great! *You* were great!"

The prince laughed warmly. "Sweetheart, it wasn't me. It was all you. You helped them come to terms with everything beautifully. I know it proved difficult, but you really succeeded brilliantly."

Misty's earlier grin grew with each of these compliments. "Thank you, sweetie! I couldn't have done it without you and Kara, though. I only hope I can help Kara find a family half as amazing as her." The smile on her face faded as the words she'd been saying took on meaning.

Derrick touched her face lightly. "About that, sweetheart—" The prince shifted position, readying himself to impart a message to her. "Maybe you shouldn't worry so much."

"What do you mean?" she asked, her forehead wrinkling in distress.

"I—um, see—" the prince hesitated.

Laughing in an effort to diffuse his stress, Misty squeezed his shoulder. "It's okay, sweetie. Tell me."

Derrick shrugged. "It's really nothing. Kara's doing extremely well with us, that's all." He stopped and took her hand. "Let's finish this conversation tomorrow. It's getting late."

"Sure. Sweet dreams, my love."

With that, she called Marie and went off to bed, delighted to be able to stay in the home she'd created in Mooncrest.

Chapter Thirteen

In the days that followed, Misty continued to enjoy the life into which she, Derrick, and Kara had fallen. Initially, she worried that living with Derrick's parents instead of her own would be incredibly strange but, to both her delight and relief, they were more than accommodating and they accepted her in the same way they did their son. As the animosity between the two families dissipated further with each passing day, Archibald took to cooking again. Misty was ecstatic to have the opportunity to not only visit her parents, but also to finally establish herself as someone with power in both Starryton and Mooncrest.

All in all, her life was currently better than it had ever been—with one exception. She still lamented Kara not having a permanent family as of yet. One particular Saturday evening found her calling another round of potential adoptive families and Derrick returning from a fishing trip he'd taken with both of their fathers.

"Hey sweetheart, have fun?" she asked cheerfully after hanging up the phone.

"Yep, we had a nice time. The day was very peaceful," he replied excitedly.

"Peaceful?" she chuckled. "That must mean Daddy refrained from any attempts to punch out your father."

The prince moved his head from right to left. "No, sweetie, your father behaved perfectly. How was your day?

Misty beamed. "Good! Kara and I had a nice breakfast, did some shopping, and got manicures." She held her hand up, proudly putting her purple nails in full view.

"Beautiful just like you," he complimented after inspecting them closely. Where's Kara now?"

"She's playing with the animals while I make some calls. I've got one more. After I'm done, how about a movie night?" she started dialing before she'd fully finished the question.

Derrick grinned conspiratorially, grabbing the phone out of her hand. "I have a better idea. Come on."

The princess laughed, her nose scrunching in conjunction with the sound. "Where ar—"

He put a finger to her lips to quiet her. "Shhh. No questions. Just follow me," he whispered.

Misty and Derrick's destination turned out to be the greenhouse, which surprised her immeasurably.

"Sweetheart, don't take this the wrong way, but it's dusk. Why are we here?" she wondered aloud.

Derrick wordlessly held the door to the greenhouse ajar, gesturing for her to go in ahead of him.

Misty gasped as she came into the space. The twinkle lights strung throughout the sea of tropical plants cast a soft glow on the garden. As she took in all of this beauty, she detected the fairy lullaby from *A Midsummer Night's Dream* playing softly. The smile that had already bloomed on her face widened as tiny purple butterflies enveloped her and Derrick in a cloud of fluttering wings.

Her eyes going wide as one of the insects landed on her shoulder, Misty breathed, "How did you do this?"

"Some butterflies are crepuscular, meaning that they fly at dawn and dusk. Obviously, these," he pointed upward and outward, "are of that variety."

"You know that's not what I mean," the princess chuckled. She lowered her voice, trying her hardest to not disturb their miniscule companions. "This is wonderfully amazing—how did you do it?" she asked, repeating her earlier question in a bright voice.

Derrick laughed in response, his gaze full of love. "You do know Prince Charming can't give away all of his secrets, right?" he beamed delightedly. "I can't tell you how, but I'll tell you why. Does that work?"

"I don't know how much of a Prince Charming you are," she joked with a giggle. "But yes, that sounds fair. Do tell."

Derrick smiled, taking her hands in his. "I asked your father a very important question today, and now I'm going to ask you a similar one in hopes that I get a positive answer." The next thing she knew, he'd gotten down on one knee and was beaming brightly up at her.

The princess inhaled a rush of air, shocked.

Derrick's face lit up at her expression and he launched in. "I love you, Misty Miles. I can't think of a person I want to spend the rest of my life with more. You'll be my perfect counterpart in reigning over this kingdom." The prince stopped to catch his breath, pulling a small box out of his pocket at the same time. His hands trembled with the magnitude of the occasion. "Will you marry me?"

If this is a dream, no one gets to pinch me, she resolved inwardly. "Of course I'll marry you!" she exclaimed.

Smiling brilliantly, the prince slid the ring onto her finger, encircling her in a fierce hug.

After a long moment, he pulled away to kiss her deeply. "I love you. I want to marry you and adopt Kara so we can officially be the family we already are."

Misty leaned in to kiss him a second time, her grin lingering long after their lips had parted. When she came back to herself, she inspected her ring. "Derrick, it's beautiful!" she gushed. The white-gold rose-cut piece had a vibrant oval amethyst with small diamond clusters surrounding it. Its appearance was remarkably delicate and feminine.

"I adore it!" the princess continued, turning the ring so that each corner caught the light.

"*You're* beautiful," Derrick insisted. "I love you."

"You really are my prince. I want nothing more than to build a family with you." Misty effused.

"Glad to hear it." Derrick touched her arm, started toward the door. Let's talk to our daughter."

* * *

Misty knocked excitedly on Kara's door once she and Derrick stood in front of it.

"Hey, where have you guys been? I thought we were going to—" Kara greeted.

"We're engaged!" the princess showed her hand, along with its new addition, to the little girl.

"I'm so happy for you!" she gushed to Misty. She turned toward Derrick. "It's about time you got yourself together."

The prince chuckled. "Hey, give me some credit. I wanted to get it right—the perfect place, the perfect ring and, of course, the perfect woman," Derrick told her.

"Can you at least let me be excited for a couple of minutes before you go all mushy on me?" she pretended to gag, rolling her eyes.

The young couple laughed. "Thanks for that, but we need to talk to you," they explained together.

"Don't worry. I'll move out right after the wedding. If there's still no family, I'll go back to the group home," Kara said, flashing a brittle grin. "You guys don't need an annoying kid around once you're newlyweds."

Misty shook her head desperately. "No, no sweetie. You couldn't be more wrong. We love having you here."

The prince nodded his support, lacing his fingers with Misty's. "You're not the most troublesome kid I've met. Just so you know," he teased. "Plus, we never see these guys," he pointed at Dex and Cliff, lounging near her, "anymore. They spend all of their time with you. They'd be devastated if you left and, honestly, Misty and I wouldn't be any better off."

The young girl giggled, making the dimples Misty had come to love appear. " Okay. I'll stay until we find a family for me, but you guys really have to swear you won't be all lovey-dovey around me."

"Kara sweetheart, we want you to do more than stay with us," the princess clarified slowly.

To accompany this, the prince extracted a small box, almost identical to the one he'd presented to Misty minutes before, from his pocket. Watching Derrick open the box and hand it to Kara, Misty knew she wasn't going to be the only girl receiving a ring that evening. He caught her eye for a heartbeat before returning his focus to Kara. "Sweetheart, we don't want to find you another place to live. You've become family and this is your home. We want you to stay, as our daughter." The prince allowed for reaction time, but the little girl had no response, so he turned things over to Misty. "Anything to add?"

"Listen to him, sweetie. You don't realize how amazing you are. You've enriched our lives so much. You're a spunky, fun little girl, who's already wise beyond her years. I can't wait to have a front-row seat to you becoming a spectacular woman." She reached for the little girl's hand, squeezing it in reassurance. "If you'll give me—us—the chance to."

Kara stared, open-mouthed, at both of them, still putting forward no verbal cues.

At that moment Misty stared at the young girl's ring wide-eyed. *Her ring has the same gemstones as the necklace Trovella used to grant my wish. That can't be a coincidence. It's a sign that we're meant to be a family,* she thought, crossing her fingers as she anxiously awaited a response.

Derrick seized his opportunity to finish their pitch. "This is for you," he offered, waving toward the ring she held. "It's an infinity symbol with a ruby, a topaz, and a sapphire in the middle of it. Our birthstones. Having them all together represents the fact that we'll be a family forever. Knowing that, will you wear it?"

Kara was sobbing before the prince could reach this conclusion. "You really want us to be a family? With me in it?" the little girl sniffled.

Derrick slipped the ring onto Kara's small finger, pulling her into a hug. "Yes, sweetie. We'd like you to be in our family," he comforted, patting her shoulder lightly before stepping aside and letting Misty do the same.

After the crying and hugging was complete, they came to the decision that the adoption should be finalized as soon as possible and that the heavy legal lifting would be done in the coming weeks. To that end, Misty and Derrick left Kara with Dex and Cliff so she could call the group home to deliver the happy news while they called Misty's parents to do the same.

Misty kissed the prince as soon as they'd stepped outside of Kara's room. "You, Derrick Denison, are amazing. That was one of the sweetest things I've ever seen."

The prince reciprocated her move, grinning through a kiss of his own. "I've got to look out for my girls. I'll take care of both of you forever," he vowed.

Chapter Fourteen

"Are you all set with those tulips, sweetheart?" Misty asked, shooting Kara a smile. "It's almost show-time."

The little girl giggled. "Shouldn't I be the one asking if you're ready for this? You are about to tie yourself to one man for the rest of your life, after all." Kara's eyes enlarged comically, stressing *life*. "All I have to do is throw some flowers on the carpet."

The princess laughed as she bent to adjust the bowtie around Dex's neck. "Don't underestimate the job—it's still tough. Don't forget, you're also about to be stuck with us." Her lips quirked upward as that thought dawned.

"How will I survive?" Kara infused her query with joyful sarcasm.

Misty started to reply, but cut off abruptly as her intro music sounded.

Smiling, she folded the little girl into her arms, and then waited as the small form walked down the aisle.

The wedding happened during a breezy April dusk in Mooncrest, at the castle greenhouse. The twinkle lights draped around the altar, constructed for the occasion, gave off an enchanting glow. Misty deemed this night more beautiful than the one on which the prince proposed, which spoke volumes regarding her happiness. Each of the hundred guests was done up beautifully, dressed to the nines and ready for a magazine cover. Most gave smiles and winks of encouragement during her journey down the aisle. However, as she made her way to her groom, he was all she saw. His gentle blue eyes contained a perfect mixture of love, admiration, and devotion.

Taking the hands he held out to her, she could only beam as the officiant, a stocky man in his early eighties with thick silver glasses and white hair, welcomed their guests, visibly overjoyed about the event he was overseeing. She tried as best she could to listen, but the only thing that registered on her consciousness was Derrick. The emotions in his eyes hypnotized her to such an extent that she missed the cue to say her vows. The prince kissed her cheek softly. "It's your turn, love."

The princess smiled, embarrassed by her inattention; taking a breath, she began her vows. "Derrick, what can I say? I love you more than I can adequately express, so I really don't know where to begin. You've shown me tremendous kindness and affection, gone out of your way to make me happy—I cannot thank you enough for that. I'll keep this short and sweet, saying only this: From this day forward, I promise to try my best to make you happy, cherishing you as much as I possibly can."

Derrick, in turn, started his vows, his eyes radiating more emotion than they had been just moments ago. "Misty, I've loved you since the day you, quite literally, stumbled into my life," he chuckled. "You've been incomparably wonderful for me and the people of this realm. You've brought more love and light into my life than I ever thought possible." He paused, allowing his words to fully resonate before continuing. "From this day on, I will devote my life to bringing as much love and light into your life as you have brought into mine."

Following this firm declaration, Derrick pressed a kiss to Misty's mouth, nodding at the officiant, who hadn't stopped smiling, to move on.

Clearing his throat, the older man proclaimed, "Ladies and gentlemen, as you may or may not know, in addition to being ordained, I also serve Mooncrest as a judge. I have many duties and responsibilities in this capacity, and none gives me greater pleasure than signing off on the adoption of children in need, thereby providing them with ameliorated circumstances."

Misty's eyes momentarily broke away from the prince's to watch Kara process the proceeding.

"I'm delighted to tell you that this already exuberant occasion will be marked by an act such as this. The loving individuals standing before you have chosen to have the first decision they make as a married couple be in the interest of another."

Beaming benevolently in Kara's direction, the preacher motioned for her to step closer to him. She did as he asked of her, facing the guests. He placed a hand on her shoulder and added, "They've chosen to adopt Kara here and will now take a moment to say a few words to her."

The prince smiled at Kara before beginning. "First off, I have to tell you that you're by far the prettiest little girl I've ever seen. I'm definitely going to have to have the kingdom guard on standby when boys start coming to the castle to take you out. Here's hoping I've got a few more years before that, though," he chuckled.

Kara giggled, rolling her eyes exaggeratedly.

"I wasn't planning on being a father for a few more years at least, but my mother always told me that the best things in life are unplanned, so I guess that's true." The prince blinked, holding back tears. "I guess what I'm trying to say is, even though your appearance in my life was unexpected, I'm going to do right by you and be the best father I can be. I can almost guarantee that you'll be the world's best daughter, though." He embraced her tightly, a single tear rolling down his cheek.

Derrick's speech had a lot more than one tear escaping from Misty's eyes. Her voice had completely faded by the time things came around to her, but she managed to overcome the obstacle. A wistful smile graced her tear-stained face as she began.

"Kara, when I first met you, you told me that you lived in Mooncrest Group Home because no one wanted you." The princess wiped fresh tears from her eyes and struggled to continue. "That's changed now. Derrick and I want nothing more than to be a part of your life, and to have you be a part of ours," she sniffled. "You deserve nothing but the best so that's what I'm going to give you," she assured affectionately, hugging the girl to her. The prince quietly inserted himself in the middle of this, creating a group hug as the fairy lullaby from *A Midsummer Night's Dream* started to play.

"Ladies and gentlemen, it is my pleasure to present Mr. and Mrs. Derrick Denison—and their daughter, Kara," the officiant announced resoundingly. Making their way up the aisle together, the new family followed the combination preacher and judge to Kingdom Hall to fill out paperwork legalizing the adoption before heading to their wedding reception to dance the night away.

* * *

Derrick and Misty came home blissful and relaxed after a week-long honeymoon in Trovella's hut. The prince had cleaned and outfitted it with the comfiest furniture and other luxurious accommodations for them.

The princess noted, with much surprise, that their parents sat together in the dining room, surrounded by piles of paperwork, fabric samples, and glittering headpieces; they appeared to be far from relaxed. She studied both royal couples intently. Archibald had dark circles under his eyes and her father looked like he could blow over with the touch of a feather. Their mothers, conversely, were both wide awake like they had spent half the night consuming energy drinks. "What's going on in here?" Misty asked.

"Oh, thank heaven. You're home! We have quite a bit to do." Her mother's features creased worriedly as she pulled her to her side.

The princess stared at her mother blankly from this new vantage point. "What are you talking about, Mama?" We haven't even been back ten minutes."

Eliza and Marguerite gaped at her with wide eyes, silently implying that the source of their stress should be extremely obvious. She looked to the kings for assistance. "Fill me in," she pleaded.

Her father roared with laughter. "The coronation, sweetheart. We're planning yours and Derrick's coronation."

Archibald nodded his agreement. "Your father and I are handling the technical aspects," he supplied, eying the women next to him. "Those two wanted to deal with the finer details."

Rolling her eyes at that comment, Eliza sighed heavily. "You gentlemen can't even begin to understand our tasks."

Marguerite laughed in encouragement. "Come along, Misty. We could use your help."

Archibald spun around, searching the space that they occupied. "Where is that son of ours? He's needed as well."

Misty paged Derrick, who materialized a few minutes later. "What's up, my darling wife?" he inquired after he'd said hello with a kiss.

"Honeymoon's over," she pouted. "You're being coerced into ironing out several snafus with our forthcoming coronation."

"I'd rather spend time with you and Kara," he whispered in her ear; he intended to add something else to the end of this, but his mother halted him by pointedly clearing her throat. "There'll be time for that later. Come, come," she insisted, pulling the princess away urgently.

Marguerite whisked Misty to her secret jewelry room; as it turned out, everything needed to host a royal extravaganza every day for the next decade, not just gems, was housed there. The princess all but lived there for the next three days, making a myriad of decisions, from the color scheme that would decorate Kingdom Hall the day of the ceremony, to the song selection the string quartet would have for the reception that was set to follow. One could almost see her relief when the day of the coronation finally arrived.

*　*　*

As she, Derrick and Kara entered Kingdom Hall just before the ceremony, she released an awed breath, happy that she'd chosen appropriate decor. A crystal chandelier that glittered like the first snow of winter served as the focal point of the room. Luminous purple orchids placed on pillars in the front and back of the room brought a hint of sophistication as well as a light floral scent into the ambiance. As their group went to the front of the room, Misty was amazed to discover that every citizen of both of their kingdoms had come to witness their triumph. Doing her best to ignore the numerous pairs of eyes on her, she schooled herself to be in the moment as her father spoke.

"Ladies and gentleman, this is indeed a historic day. Many years ago, an unspeakable evil tore the beloved kingdom of Starrycrest asunder. The individuals you see before you have avenged that evil and, in doing so, have once again established unity in Starryton and Mooncrest. Today, we are here to recognize their strength by proudly coming together as a single kingdom for the second, and with any luck, final time. It is with immense gratitude that I tell you the kingdoms of Starryton and Mooncrest exist no longer. As of this moment, we will join together, bringing a new and improved Starrycrest into the next century. Reginald smiled indulgently at Misty and Derrick before looking at Archibald, who nodded at him in approval.

"I thought this day would never come but, now that it has, I couldn't be happier. Without further ado—" Misty's father-in-law's eyes twinkled as he indicated that the prince should kneel before him.

Archibald patted Marguerite's arm lovingly, cleared his throat, and looked down at their son. "Do you, Derrick Denison, swear to govern the kingdom of Starrycrest according to the statutes agreed upon by those who came before you, and to protect the land and its people from potential threats by your just laws?"

The prince's eyes shown as he answered, "I so swear."

Misty's pounding heart almost prevented her from hearing her mother's recital of the same question.

After a moment, the princess's head cleared and she took Derrick's hand, "I so swear."

With that, Eliza placed a tiara on her head just as Archibald placed a crown on Derrick's. The headpieces secured, Derrick stood and he and Misty fixed their attention on Kara. Eyes filling with happy tears, Misty presented the little girl with a question. "Do you, Kara Denison, solemnly swear to learn all you can about the statues and governing practices of the kingdom of Starrycrest in the capacity of princess?"

Kara smiled brightly. "I so swear," she chorused happily. The young couple beamed as they listened to their daughter; when she'd finished, they both leaned in and hugged her. Eventually, after expressions had been composed, the seven members of the royal family faced their people and Derrick addressed the crowd. "Ladies and gentlemen, the coronation you've just witnessed brings a new day to the kingdom of Starrycrest. By royal decree, this day shall now and forevermore be deemed a royal holiday, to be marked by joyous celebration."

With that, he led everyone to his and Misty's reception for a night of food, fun, and dancing. From that day forward, Derrick, Misty, Kara and every citizen of Starrycrest, from infants to great-grandparents, lived happily ever after.

About the Author

Allison M. Lewis (Boot), otherwise known as the Wheelin' Wordsmith, wrote this story to spread a message of self-acceptance to young adults and children traveling paths similar to hers. She earned a Master of Arts in Mass Communication from the University of Dayton and currently resides in Urbana, Illinois with her husband, Dylan. She is also the owner of an extensive troll doll collection, started at the tender age of three, after being told that they bring good luck. To this day, it continues to grow and do just that.

Want to Connect with The Wheelin' Wordsmith?

Join her mailing list by visiting www.allisonmbootauthor.com, where you can learn more about her and her books today! Also, don't forget to "like" her on Facebook and Pinterest as well as follow her on Twitter at @WheelNWordsmith and Instagram at @Wheelin_Wordsmith

Made in United States
Orlando, FL
31 July 2024